DELIVERANCE

ANNE SCHRAFF

SADDLEBACK
EDUCATIONAL PUBLISHING

2/13
PA

URBAN UNDERGROUND

SADDLEBACK
EDUCATIONAL PUBLISHING
www.sdlback.com

ISBN-13: 978-1-61651-587-4
ISBN-10: 1-61651-587-2
eBook: 978-1-61247-233-1

Printed in Guangzhou, China
0212/CA21200288

16 15 14 13 12   1 2 3 4 5

CHAPTER ONE

Sixteen-year-old Naomi Martinez rushed from Chill Out. She had been working at the yogurt shop for two weeks. Sherry Carranza, the crew leader, said Naomi was the best worker they ever had. She was efficient and friendly. The customers loved her. The owner of Chill Out was Elia Ancho. When Mr. Ancho first saw Naomi, he had told his son Jimmy she was "stunning."

Naomi's boyfriend, Ernesto Sandoval, was waiting in his Volvo. He had parked in the Chill Out parking lot to take her home. Naomi and Ernesto were juniors at Cesar Chavez High School. Ernesto had been born in the *barrio*. But he and his family had spent ten years in Los Angeles. Then Luis Sandoval, Ernesto's father, got a job teaching history at Chavez. So they came back to the *barrio*. Ernesto and Naomi had been dating ever since then.

"I got my paycheck," Naomi said, ripping open the envelope. "Oh, I love payday!"

"I hear you, babe," Ernesto agreed. "When it's payday at the pizzeria, I'm happy. Now that I'm the assistant manager, the check is a little fatter. All good!"

"Ernie!" Naomi cried, "I got a raise already. I've been there only two weeks, and I got a raise!"

"Is it a good one?" Ernesto asked, smiling at Naomi. She was probably the most beautiful girl at Chavez High. She was the most beautiful girl Ernesto ever saw. That was for sure. She had awesome violet eyes and perfect features. Her skin was a lovely creamy coffee brown, and she was slim. She looked irresistible in a sweater and skinny jeans.

"Ernie, it's huge!" she exclaimed. "I can't believe this! It's almost double what I was getting. This is amazing."

"Wow, they must like you a lot, Naomi," Ernesto remarked, as he pulled the Volvo out of the parking lot.

"Well, Sherry, the team leader, is always telling me how good I am," Naomi explained. "And Jimmy Ancho, the boss's son, he's the manager. He's saying good things too, but I never expected this! What do I do? Thank them?"

"Sure, but don't go overboard," Ernesto advised. "Don't get all emotional about the size of the raise. They might think maybe they made a mistake and gave you too much. You just say, 'Thanks a lot for the raise.' Give them a real cool smile. Let it go at that. Then they'll think you *know* you're good. They'll feel lucky to have you."

"Oh Ernie, I've been saving for a car of my own," Naomi told him. "I'd love a nice sporty car to run around in. Daddy wants me to drive the old family sedan. But I hate that old Toyota. I want something like Carmen's car. I saw one for sale for under two thousand. Wow, making this kind of money, I'd have enough in no time."

Naomi's eyes widened. "You don't think they made a mistake on my paycheck, do you? I mean, it's hard to believe. Would they give me that big of a raise so soon?"

Ernesto looked over at Naomi and grinned. "Don't even think that, babe. If you even breathe something like that, you're cooked. Let's say they did make a mistake. If you thank them, then they'll have to let you keep it. They'll be ashamed to take the money back."

"You know, Ernie," Naomi commented. "It's such fun working there. It's like not even work. The customers are so nice. Sherry is great. Jimmy is so friendly. I don't have much to do with the dad. But I can tell even he likes me. He always notices me and gives me a big smile. He'll come in sometimes. He just sits there at his favorite table for half the night. I guess he likes to make sure everything is going okay."

"Well, Naomi, you deserve a break," Ernesto told her. "You really went all-out arranging that fiftieth birthday party for your dad. That was so awesome. To think your brothers hadn't seen him in years. Yet you managed to work it out so all that bitterness was erased. Your dad and his boys are reconciled. That was beautiful, Naomi. And you did it all. How's it working out now? Are Orlando and Manny coming around a lot?"

Naomi giggled. "Well, they both work in LA, of course. So they don't live at the house anymore. But you know what? About every two weeks, they come home. They sleep over in their own bedroom. Then they're in there like little boys roughhousing. They're just like they used to be when they were kids! It's like all those horrible years have disappeared. It means the world to Mom, and it just was like salvation for Dad."

Naomi paused a moment to think. "Breakfast is the best time," she said.

"There we are, all six of us. We're just sitting around the breakfast table yakking. The boys got home last night. Ernie, it's like a light goes on in Dad's eyes."

For years, Orlando and Manny had been unforgiven and unreconciled with Dad. During those years, there had always been a heavy darkness in the Martinez house. It was as if heavy curtains were always drawn shut and no light could come in. Anyone could feel the ill will between Felix Martinez and his missing sons. Now the little house on Bluebird Street seemed lighter and brighter.

"I've seen your dad a few times," Ernesto commented. "Now that your brothers are back in the family circle, it's like a big load was lifted off your dad's shoulders. Being estranged from his two boys all that time must have hurt a lot. I know he threw them out. But I think he figured they'd come crawling right back. And they might've *never* come back if you hadn't worked it out, Naomi."

"Daddy and Orlando still argue," Naomi remarked. "But they end up making fun of each other and laughing now. It makes me so happy."

Ernesto pulled into the Martinez driveway. Dad and Orlando were in front playing with Brutus, the family's pit bull. Both Orlando and Manny would be at the house until tomorrow night. Then they'd board the Oscar Perez Latin Band bus and head for Los Angeles again. Orlando was a singer. Manny usually took care of the equipment and sometimes played the guitar.

"Hey, Naomi! Ernie!" Orlando yelled. "Look at this dog. I've only been with him a couple hours in the last few weeks. Already he loves me."

"Hey," Dad protested, "Brutus loves everybody. Don't get a big head, Orlando. This is the sweetest dog in the world."

"I don't know," Orlando teased. "Pit bulls usually have their favorites. And I think I'm Brutus's favorite."

"Look at this kid," Dad complained. He was making believe he was annoyed. "He's been around here a couple, three weeks. Already he's stealing the affection of my dog away from me!"

"Daddy, Orlando, I got a huge raise down at Chill Out," Naomi announced. "Look at my paycheck!"

Dad and Orlando looked at the check. Orlando remarked, "That's a lot of money for dishing out yogurt, sis. Way to go!"

"Yeah," Naomi agreed, "I'm saving for my own car. This is going to help a lot."

"We got a perfectly good Toyota Camry sitting in the garage," Dad said. "I use the pickup all the time. The Camry's like new. But no, the girl wants to be tooling around town in something sportier. Naomi, look at your boyfriend here. Look at Ernie. He drives the ugliest car in the *barrio*. An old granny Volvo. And still you love him."

Orlando threw back his head and laughed. "You gotta get a different car, Ernie. Dad's right. Your car is not cool."

"Well," Ernesto squirmed, "the thing is, the car works like a charm. It never needs repairs. It just goes and goes. I'm sort of attached to it now. It's like a faithful old horse. I'd feel disloyal getting rid of it. I mean, it's been so reliable. I'd hate to send her to the crusher."

"I like this guy, Naomi," Orlando commented. "He's sentimental about a car. He has compassion for a Volvo. You can't go wrong with a guy like this."

Naomi kissed Ernesto good-bye and went into the house. She was about to throw out her paycheck envelope when she noticed a piece of paper inside it. She took the paper out and read it. It said, "Naomi, I just wanted you to know that your work at Chill Out is extraordinary. I hope you know you are appreciated. Elia Ancho."

Naomi was stunned. The older man had spent hours sitting at that table observing her. And he thought she was good enough for that big raise. Naomi had assumed Sherry told Jimmy what a good job Naomi was doing. Then Jimmy approved the raise. It was amazing to her that Elia Ancho was so hands-on.

At work after school the next day, Naomi looked for Mr. Ancho to thank him. But he wasn't at his usual table. Mr. Ancho was a handsome man, about sixty, silver haired and distinguished looking. He looked as though he might be a university professor, a scientist, or someone who conducted an orchestra.

Naomi was uncertain whether she should wait for Mr. Ancho. She wanted to thank him personally because he'd left her the complimentary note. She could just thank Jimmy, his son. Probably the two of them had discussed the raise and agreed on it. Naomi felt a little funny about sharing the news of the raise with Sherry. She was afraid maybe Sherry wasn't paid as well. Maybe she'd be jealous. Naomi didn't want any hard feelings that might jeopardize this job she loved so much.

CHAPTER ONE

When Jimmy Ancho came in, Naomi approached him. Jimmy was a nice-looking guy, about twenty-five. He was the one who actually hired Naomi.

"Mr. Ancho," Naomi began.

"I'm not *Mr.* Ancho," Jimmy objected with a smile. "My father is Mr. Ancho. I'm Jimmy."

"Oh . . . okay," Naomi said. "I just wanted to thank you for the raise. Your father gave me a nice note in my pay envelope, praising my work. I wanted to thank him personally. But I don't see him yet."

Jimmy looked surprised. He stared at Naomi for a second. Then he said, "I didn't even know you got a raise. Dad did that on his own apparently. But you *are* a darn good employee, Naomi. I know that."

"Thank you very much, Jimmy," Naomi replied.

"Course," Jimmy added with a wry smile, "it helps that you're such eye candy. A lotta dudes come in here for a look at the babe as much as for the frozen yogurt. But that's fine. They buy yogurt too."

Naomi didn't know what to say. She felt uncomfortable. So she mumbled, "Well, I really enjoy working here."

Some customers *did* flirt with Naomi during the evening shift. But she handled them very professionally. She offered good service and a friendly smile to everyone, from the little old ladies to the young dudes.

Late in her shift, Elia Ancho came in. He went to his favorite table. He seemed to be looking intently at Naomi. Every time she glanced in his direction, he was looking at her. Naomi thought he might be waiting for her to thank him personally for the raise. Right after her shift ended, she walked to his table and spoke to him. "Mr. Ancho, I got your note. I really appreciate your kind words."

"And we appreciate you," he responded.

"Thank you so much for the generous raise," Naomi added.

CHAPTER ONE

"I believe that quality workers deserve to be rewarded," he told her. "A lot of young people don't have a work ethic like yours. You're mature beyond your years. I noticed at once that you were exceptional. Looking at your employment application, I expected you were much older, perhaps eighteen. I was surprised that you are only sixteen. I've observed you with many customers. A few of them were quite rude. They paid you attention that I'm sure you didn't want. But you were splendid."

Naomi remembered the time Clay Aguirre came into Chill Out. He made rude, gross comments. But Naomi treated him just like any other customer.

"I'll be seventeen in the spring," was all she could say in response.

"Well, I'm very glad you're working here," the man told her. His clear blue eyes focused on Naomi in a way that made her feel uncomfortable. He must have been extremely handsome when he was younger. He was still fine looking. His face was tanned and remarkably unlined. And he had chiseled features.

Naomi walked out into the dark parking lot behind the store. That was where Ernesto usually was waiting. She looked around for his Volvo. He was never late in picking her up. Usually he was at least ten minutes early. But now he was nowhere in sight. Naomi had turned off her cell phone during her shift. That was the rule. Now she turned it on. There might be a message from Ernesto. Perhaps his faithful Volvo had finally broken down.

Ernesto *had* left a voice mail.

"Naomi," the message went, "I got a text message from someone. It said you were going home with somebody from work. Call me if that's not right."

Naomi was puzzled. She called Ernesto immediately. "Ernie, I didn't plan to go home with anybody else. I don't know who sent you that message."

"Okay, babe," Ernesto responded. "Stay in a safe place. I'll be there in five minutes."

Naomi glanced across the parking lot. Sometimes her former boyfriend, Clay Aguirre, parked there. He hoped to see Naomi and start a conversation. Once or twice he even offered to drive her home. At one time, Naomi had cared a lot for Clay, even though he was often rude to her. Then once, after a big argument, he punched her in the face. That ended their relationship. Naomi broke with him for good.

Now Naomi spotted Clay's Mustang parked near the dumpsters. Naomi was enraged. It would be just like Clay to have sent Ernesto that message. Clay could then get Naomi into his car to talk about getting back together. "Old Ernie stand you up, babe?" he called to her. "I can give you a ride home."

"Clay, what are you doing here? Ernie's coming. He'll be here in a minute," Naomi replied coldly. She wondered. Was Clay deluded enough to go that far?

"You know what?" Clay told her. "If I had a beautiful chick like you waiting on

15

me, I wouldn't be late picking her up. I don't think the dude appreciates you, girl. I mean, stranding you in a dark, dangerous place like this. You got gangbangers walking down this street."

"It was a misunderstanding," Naomi explained. "Some creep texted Ernie that I didn't need a ride."

The door to Chill Out swung open. Mr. Ancho stood there for a moment. "Is everything all right?" he asked Naomi. "Didn't your ride come?"

"He's a little late," Naomi answered. "He'll be here any minute."

Mr. Ancho came closer. He glanced over at Clay Aguirre. "This punk isn't bothering you, is he?" he asked.

"Oh no, it's okay," Naomi said quickly. "He's a student at Chavez High. I know him."

"I don't like the looks of him," Mr. Ancho remarked.

"No, it's okay," Naomi assured him nervously.

"If you have any problem getting home, I'd be most happy to take you," Mr. Ancho offered. "My BMW is parked right over there. This isn't the best of neighborhoods for a young lady like yourself to be alone."

"That's very kind of you, Mr. Ancho," Naomi replied. "But I see my ride coming now. The Volvo. See, it's pulling up."

"All right then," Mr. Ancho said, returning to Chill Out. A moment later he opened the heavy metal back door again. He wanted to make sure Naomi was getting into the car. Then he closed it.

The Volvo slowed to a stop next to Naomi, and she got in. "Ernie," Naomi remarked, "that's so weird. Why would somebody lie that I had a ride home? Do you know who texted you? Clay was hanging around again. I thought maybe he did it so he could take me home."

"Maybe it was him," Ernesto mused, "but I don't think so. He's still trying to get you back. But he knows I'd be on him real quick if I found out he did something like that."

"Who could have done it then?" Naomi wondered aloud. She felt vulnerable that somebody would want to cancel her ride for some reason.

"Beats me," Ernesto said. "Okay, I'm not gonna believe that kind of message again. I'm gonna be here to get you, Naomi, no matter what. I wonder if somebody from school is hanging around Chill Out? Maybe somebody's scheming to get something going with you? A lot of guys know my cell phone number. I've been in Chill Out a coupla times since you've been working here."

Ernesto was quiet for a while, thinking. "I saw Jorge Aguilar really staring at you, Naomi," he finally said. "He's on the track team with me, but I don't know him too well. He told me a couple times that he thinks you're really hot. Aguilar's okay, I guess, but I wouldn't put a stunt like that past him."

"I don't even know him," Naomi commented. "Besides, why wasn't *he* there to pick me up?"

Ernesto shook his head as if to say, "I don't know." Then he said, "Trouble is you're so darn beautiful, Naomi. You know, even that old guy, the boss's father. I've seen him sitting at that table in the corner just staring at you. He gives me the creeps."

"Yeah, I know," she agreed. "He's extra nice to me. I feel a little weird about that too. But he's an honorable older man. He just wouldn't pull some stunt like canceling my ride so he could take me home!"

Naomi tried to remember Jorge Aguilar coming into Chill Out. She had seen him run during the track meets. But she never really talked to him much. Now that she thought about it, though, she remembered something. He once told her he didn't need any sugar for his coffee. He said Naomi was so sweet she should just put her finger in the coffee and stir.

CHAPTER TWO

After Naomi got home, she kept thinking about the phony message Ernesto got. Maybe it was Clay Aguirre. It made sense to Naomi that Clay would do such a thing. He wasn't giving up on getting Naomi back. He wasn't facing the truth that she was so over him. She could barely stand to see his face anymore. Besides, she cared deeply for Ernesto Sandoval.

Orlando and Manny had stayed for dinner. Ernesto left for home but offered to drive them down to Hortencia's around nine. The Perez bus was parked there. For now, the entire Martinez family was sitting around the dinner table. They were just like in the old days before the bitter rift had happened. Felix Martinez looked around the table. His heart swelled with pride and joy to see his three sons and daughter, all together at his table.

Naomi had also noticed something dramatically different about Dad since the two older boys were back. Before, Dad had often been very critical of Mom's cooking. He thought nothing of describing the food on the table as "slop." Naomi often saw the hurt in her mother's eyes. Now, Dad was much nicer. He hated vegetables, but tonight Mom served roasted winter vegetables and cheesy polenta. She'd begun watching cooking shows on TV, and she was experimenting with new dishes. Things had changed for the better in the Martinez household.

Naomi rode her bike to school the next day. She was chaining it to the bike stand just as Ernesto jogged up. He liked to jog in the nice weather, Jogging strengthened his legs for track and was fun. They strolled toward their first class.

"Did my brothers get off okay last night on the bus?" Naomi asked.

"Yeah, the big bus was sitting there at Hortencia's," he reported. "Oscar Perez and *Tía* Hortencia, they were hot and heavy until the last minute. The driver had to honk to get Oscar on the bus. You know, Naomi, as I was taking the guys over there, Manny said something. He said you got a real nice soprano voice."

When Naomi was a young teenager, she enjoyed singing with her brothers in the garage band. They did little gigs for friends' birthdays but nothing for money. That seemed like a very long time ago to Naomi.

"Naomi," Ernesto asked, "we're having a special program honoring Cesar Chavez on his birthday. Tryouts are being held here at school. There's a role for a guy to give some of the speeches Chavez gave. It's just a speaking part, and I'm thinking of trying out for it. I'd be playing Chavez. But then they need a girl with a nice voice to be

Dolores Huerta. She needs to sing just one song and—"

"No way," Naomi cut him off quickly. "I'm putting in a lot of hours at Chill Out, and I got my homework. I wouldn't have time for anything like that."

"It really wouldn't be that much work," Ernesto explained. "Orlando and Manny said they'd help you. It's just going to be a one-night program at school."

"Ernie, why are you so interested in this?" Naomi asked.

"Uh well, I thought it'd be fun for us to work together," Ernesto replied.

"Come on, Ernie. What's really going on?" Naomi persisted.

"I'd like for us to work together," he said again. Naomi just stared at him. "And I'd like for you to sing that song. I'd like to have everybody see what a good singer you are. Your folks would be really proud."

Naomi sighed. "Well, I'll think about it. When are the tryouts?"

"In about two weeks," Ernesto answered eagerly. "Angelina D'Cruz, she's our music and drama teacher here at school. She's putting it all together, and it's gonna be really beautiful."

"Well," Naomi consented, "maybe I'll try out, but I won't get it. I'm not a singer like Orlando. He's really good. I was okay for our dumb little garage band. But this is different."

"Well let's see what happens," Ernesto suggested.

Naomi changed the subject. "Have you figured out yet who texted you about not picking me up, Ernie? I keep thinking about that. The thought makes me uneasy."

"Now I'm thinking Clay Aguirre was behind it," Ernesto answered. "If he called, I'd have recognized his voice. So he texted. He's thinking constantly of how to get back into your life. Maybe he figures you'll change your mind if you're riding home with him in that Mustang. Maybe all the old feelings will come back."

"Yeah, I think you're right about him," Naomi agreed. "I'm telling you, Ernie, if Clay does one more weird thing, I'm reporting him to the police. He sometimes parks outside my house at night and shines a flashlight at my window. I can't take it. I'm getting one of those restraining orders or something if he doesn't keep away from me."

"Look," Ernesto said, "there he is now. He's just standing there, staring over in this direction. Naomi, I'm gonna talk to the guy one more time. He never had any respect for me until that incident with Julio Avila. Remember, me and Abel stopped Julio from taking Clay on with the switchblade? Since then, Clay has listened a little more to what I have to say. Let me give it one more shot before you go to the police."

"Okay," Naomi replied. "Good luck." She went on to her first class.

Ernesto crossed the campus to where Clay Aguirre stood.

"Hey man," Ernesto hailed him. "I need to talk to you about something that's real important. For your own good, hear me out?"

Clay usually sneered when Ernesto approached him and tossed out some insult. But now Clay just stood there. "Yeah? What's up?" he asked.

"You're scaring Naomi by hanging around her job, her house," Ernesto advised him. "You're scaring the girl. And it's got to stop right now, Clay."

"I'm not doing anything wrong," Clay snapped.

"Last night you were parked at Chill Out when she came off work," Ernesto told him. "When I wasn't there to pick her up right away, you tried taking her home. That's got to stop."

"I was in Chill Out getting some frozen yogurt," Clay protested. "I just happened to see her standing there without a ride. Don't tell me Chill Out's off limits to me just because she works there. That's crazy, dude."

"You go there and get your yogurt. Then move on," Ernesto commanded Clay.

CHAPTER TWO

"No more sitting in the parking lot, waiting for her. And another thing. Something really weird happened last night. Somebody texted me that I didn't need to pick Naomi up. Whoever it was said she got a ride with somebody else. Did you have something to do with that, Clay? Did you text me so that you could take Naomi home?"

Clay looked indignant. "I didn't have anything to do with that, dude. I don't know what you're talking about." Ernesto couldn't tell whether Clay was telling the truth or blowing smoke.

"Here's the deal man," Ernesto said in a harsh voice. "Don't you be parking at Chill Out waiting for her. Don't you be parking across from her house. You got that? Just go about your business man. You just deal with the fact that she doesn't want anything to do with you anymore. You're scaring Naomi. If you don't bug off man, she's going to report you to the cops as a stalker. That's a bad rap man. You got fair warning."

Clay's eyes narrowed. "You put her up to that stalker garbage, didn't you, Sandoval?" Clay snarled. "You're so scared she's gonna come to her senses and dump you. You need the cops to help you keep me and Naomi apart."

"Just listen to me, Clay. Leave her alone," Ernesto commanded in a calm voice.

"You think I'm the only guy who hangs around Naomi?" Clay responded. "She's a hot chick. Plenty guys got their eye on her. When she's playing volleyball here at school, I see guys drooling. I hear cracks about her from a lot of guys. She's hot man, and I'm not the only one seeing that."

"Yeah," Ernesto granted. "But you're the only one parked outside her house and sitting in the parking lot at Chill Out. I'm not wasting any more time with you, dude. Naomi doesn't want to see that Mustang parked there when she comes off work. She doesn't want to look out her bedroom window and see you with the flashlight."

"Okay," Clay Aguirre relented. "Tell her she's making the mistake of her life. She's giving up a guy who loved her more than anybody in the world. But okay, I'm done. Tell her I'm over her. Tell her if she gets on her knees and begs me to take her back, I won't. It's over. It's done." With that, Clay Aguirre turned and walked away.

Carmen Ibarra came along. She was a good friend of Ernesto's and the daughter of just elected councilman Emilio Zapata Ibarra. She had seen Ernesto and Clay arguing. "What was that all about, Ernie?" she asked. "I could hear you guys yelling way over in the parking lot."

"Clay Aguirre doesn't understand what 'no' means," Ernesto explained. "Naomi doesn't want him in her life anymore. But he keeps parking at her house, hanging at her work. She's getting scared. You hear about people who're like obsessed with somebody. Sometimes it gets dangerous. I just told the guy to leave Naomi alone or she's getting him busted for stalking her."

"Yeah, in class he's always staring at her," Carmen remarked. She laughed. "But then a lot of guys stare at Naomi. She's beyond pretty. When Paul Morales said I was hot, I couldn't believe that a cute guy thought *I* was hot. But every dude here at Chavez thinks Naomi's hot. I guess most of the guys would go for Naomi in a heartbeat if they could."

Ernesto then told Carmen about the text he had gotten. He explained the message telling him Naomi didn't need her usual ride. "I think Clay had something to do with that, but I'm not sure," he concluded.

"Didn't you recognize the number on your phone from the text?" Carmen asked.

"No," Ernesto replied. "It didn't look familiar. But I figured Clay got somebody else to send the text. He's got a lot of friends who'd do that for him."

"You still got it on your phone?" Carmen asked.

"Yeah, I do," Ernesto said, taking out his phone.

"Let me see it, Ernie," Carmen suggested. "Maybe I'll recognize the number."

Ernesto showed Carmen the text. She didn't recognize the number. "That's not Clay," she agreed. "The text is dorky. It sounds like a guy who doesn't know her that well. He used her full name. A kid wouldn't do that. I hope some old guy isn't coming into that yogurt place and taking a liking to Naomi. I mean, Clay's a nuisance, but I don't think he'd ever be dangerous. But what if some guy—like in his twenties—has the hots for her and is plotting to pick her up. That would worry me."

"Yeah," Ernesto said. Carmen Ibarra was smart. She noticed things Ernesto didn't. Now what she'd said really scared him. If some stranger was trying to get Naomi into his car, she might be in real danger.

"It couldn't be someone at work, could it?" Carmen asked.

"Well, she's got this young boss, Jimmy. But he seems okay," Ernesto answered.

"Naomi told me he's really cute, and he likes the girls," Carmen said. "Naomi told me about when she applied for that job at Chill Out. There were half a dozen applicants, mostly girls. When Jimmy saw Naomi, he just hired her and told everybody else the job was filled. Could Jimmy have a crush on Naomi, Ernie? I mean, it might be innocent enough if he did pull that thing about her pickup. He might have thought he'd keep you away and have a chance to take her home. Maybe he thought he could get something started with her. It doesn't necessarily mean he's some bad person or anything, Ernie. Guys sometimes do stupid things to get close to a girl they like."

"Yeah, I guess," Ernesto admitted.

"It wouldn't be the first time a guy hit on a girl who worked for him," Carmen continued. "I don't think Naomi knows much about Jimmy Ancho. He told her his dad bought the yogurt shop for him because he couldn't find a job. They're not from around here. Jimmy Ancho was born in Mexico, but he went to school in the States. I guess the dad's wealthy. Naomi said Jimmy told her his father has a lot of property in Mexico."

Ernesto frowned. "I'd want Naomi to quit that job if Jimmy Ancho has the hots for her. He's a guy like twenty-five or something. She's only a sixteen-year-old girl. I don't like the sound of that."

"Of course, we're just making wild guesses, Ernie," Carmen said. "Besides, how could Jimmy Ancho have gotten your phone number to text you?"

"Yeah!" Ernesto exclaimed, relieved by that thought. "That's true. It had to be Clay. Clay got some dude to send the text, and that's that."

You know, Carmen," Ernesto went on. "I'm trying to get Naomi to try out for that musical program honoring Cesar Chavez's birthday. I think she'd be perfect to play Dolores Huerta. When Naomi was about thirteen, she sang with her brothers in a little garage band. Her brother Orlando said she has a clear, sweet soprano. I told her I was trying out to be Cesar Chavez and it'd be great if we could work together." Ernesto had not told Carmen or anyone else the real reason he wanted Naomi in that musical celebration.

CHAPTER THREE

That would be so cool," Carmen answered enthusiastically. "Naomi would make a wonderful Dolores. Oh, I hope she does it."

Ernesto looked at Carmen. He recalled when he'd returned from Los Angeles and started attending Cesar Chavez High School. He felt like a stranger. He'd been gone from the *barrio*, where he was born, for ten years. All his friends were in Los Angeles. At Chavez, two students reached out to Ernesto. They helped him through those awful early days. One was Abel Ruiz, and the other was Carmen Ibarra.

"Thanks for being such a good friend, Carmen," Ernesto told her with feeling.

"I always know where to go when I need a shoulder to lean on."

Carmen laughed. "When I first saw you, Ernesto Sandoval, I wanted a lot more than your head on my shoulder," she admitted. "I almost fell in love with you. In fact, I didn't completely get over you until I fell for Paul Morales."

"You and Paul are a great match," he told her.

Ernesto smiled at her and started to walk to his first class. He was hoping he had convinced Naomi to try out for the Cesar Chavez program. He wasn't sure she bought his excuse for pushing her so hard to try out. He told Naomi he just wanted the pleasure of working with her on the project. But there was more to it than that. Ernesto would, of course, enjoy working with Naomi on anything. But he had another reason for Naomi to play Dolores Huerta.

A few days ago, Ernesto had stopped at Hortencia's tamale shop for one of her great green corn *tamales*. There he spotted Felix

Martinez sitting alone in a booth. Then he had a conversation with Naomi's dad that he could never have foreseen.

"Hi Mr. Martinez," Ernesto called out to him in a friendly voice. Ernesto always tried hard to be nice to Naomi's father. They had a history of problems. Mr. Martinez never liked Ernesto as his daughter's boyfriend as much as he had liked Clay Aguirre. Ernesto seemed like a wimp to Naomi's father. But Clay was a football player and a macho guy, the kind of a male that Felix Martinez respected. Lately, though, Naomi's father was warming up to Ernesto.

"Hey Ernie," Felix Martinez called. "You got a minute?"

"Sure," Ernesto said, getting his *tamale* on a tray and joining Mr. Martinez in the booth.

"Ernie, we've had our ups and downs, you and me," Mr. Martinez began. "I had it in for you a few times. Like when you worked for Emilio Ibarra to take the city council seat away from my cousin Monte. That made me mad. But, I gotta admit, you're a pretty good kid. I trust you with Naomi. My little girl, she's real precious to me. And I trust you with her."

"Thank you, sir," Ernesto replied, wondering what was coming next.

"I ain't got nobody else to talk like this to," he continued. "Linda, she's a good woman. But she starts crying at the drop of a hat. Zack, he's a good kid, but he's not very deep. For a long time, I figured Zack was my best kid. I sorta wrote off Orlando and Manny. I never thought, you know, they'd come back. And Naomi, she got to be one of those *Zapatistas*. They helped that bum Ibarra knock my cousin off the city council."

Felix Martinez took a gulp of hot coffee. His *tamale* was only half eaten. Usually he gobbled them down quickly. "The thing of it is, Ernie, turns out little Naomi is the treasure in this family. My little girl—a little slip of a thing—doesn't weigh much more than a buck ten. Only sixteen years old, she hatches this whole thing for my birthday. Linda, she was scared to do anything to rock the boat. Zack, well, he never starts nothin' that might be upsetting to somebody."

The man took another swig of coffee. He nudged the *tamale* dish an inch or two away from him. "But Naomi, she took it all on herself. She risked the whole thing blowing up in her face. She got Orlando and Manny down here, healed that terrible wound we had. Naomi got the boys to reach out to me. None of this woulda happened except for her. I been grieving for Orlando and Manny for so long. Nobody did nothin' but Naomi. It just blows me away what she did, Ernie."

Ernesto nodded in agreement. "Naomi is a very special person. Everybody sees how beautiful she is. But underneath, that's her real beauty. She's beautiful on the outside, but she's much more beautiful on the inside."

"She made our family whole again, Ernie," Mr. Martinez declared, looking Ernesto directly in the eye. "She musta been so scared. She didn't know if I'd do something stupid and blow everything. Or maybe Orlando would back out at the last minute. She was dealing with some hard-headed, stubborn dudes, but she toughed it out. It's so great with the boys home, with the anger gone. I wake up in the morning, and it's like a big ton of bricks are off my chest."

Mr. Martinez finished his coffee and got down to business. "Anyway, this is the deal, Ernie. I want for Naomi to have a chance to shine like the boys do with that Oscar Perez band. The other day I met this teacher from Chavez. She was in the super-market, and we got to talking. Name is Angelina D'Cruz."

"Yes, I know her," Ernesto responded. "She's good."

"She was telling me," Mr. Martinez said, "they're putting on this big celebration for Cesar Chavez's birthday, you know. She said they need a special girl to play this Dolores Huerta, who was like Chavez's sidekick, you know? I remembered Naomi singing with her brothers, and she sounded like an angel. I promised this D'Cruz lady I'd try to get her to try out for the celebration. Well, I thought she'd listen to you better than me, Ernie. And you could try out to be this grape guy, Chavez. You'd be good, Ernie. Can you see what you can do? Can you get my little girl to have the confidence to go to the tryouts, Ernie?"

"I'll do what I can," Ernesto promised.

"This is gonna be a big deal at school, Ernie," Felix Martinez went on. "The girl playing Dolores, she's gonna stand there in the spotlight. She'll be singing this song about the kids. It's a beautiful song. It's called "*Por los niños.*" I can just see Naomi standing there, everybody applauding. My boys, Orlando and Manny, they perform even in Las Vegas. They're big shots. But I want something special for Naomi. She deserves something like that, everybody seeing how wonderful she is."

"I'll get right on it," Ernesto pledged.

"Thanks Ernie," Mr. Martinez said. "You're okay, Ernie. You're a good kid." He clapped Ernesto on the shoulder and got up from the booth. He paid his bill and left the shop. Ernesto sat stunned at the talk he'd just had with the man.

So that was why Ernesto had pushed Naomi. Felix Martinez wanted desperately to see his daughter in the celebration as Dolores Huerta.

Soon after Mr. Martinez had made his request, Ernesto had gone to Angelina D'Cruz. He signed up to try out for the role of Cesar Chavez. He did some research on Dolores Huerta, a beautiful young woman. Well, Naomi fit the role so far. Huerta worked with Cesar Chavez at the Community Service Organization to help poor Mexican people. When Chavez started to recruit farmworkers to join a union and fight for their rights, Dolores was at his side. She worked day and night for justice. Ernesto could see Naomi putting the passion of her own heart into the role. All Ernesto had to do was convince her to go for it.

At lunch that day, Ernesto didn't sit with his regular friends—Abel, Julio, Carlos Negrete, and Dom Reynosa. He went looking for Naomi. She usually got together with Carmen Ibarra, Yvette Ozono, and Tessie Zamora. He found the girls in a shady spot under some eucalyptus trees.

"You guys," Ernesto asked sheepishly, "I just got this turkey and cheese sandwich from the vending machine. Can I join you?"

"Look who comes over and just sits down like he owns the place," Carmen teased, laughing. "The guys must have thrown him out. Now the girls are good enough for him. Dude, this is a girls-only lunch party."

"Sorry," Ernesto apologized and turned to leave. Yvette turned to him and smiled.

"Oh, come on! You can join us anytime you want, Ernie," she told him. Yvette had been a school dropout with a tragic past. Ernie and his father, Luis Sandoval, helped her get back in school. Now she was a math genius with a nice boyfriend. Tessie was healing from a bad auto accident. Now she needed only one crutch.

"Man, this is a terrible sandwich," Ernesto remarked. He had taken one bite, and that was all he wanted. "I think they must have made it a month ago. The bread is stale, and the turkey is like wood. I guess this yellow stuff is cheese, but it doesn't taste like it."

"Poor baby!" Carmen sympathized. "Luckily I have an extra yogurt. I hope you like lemon."

"Thanks, Carmen," Ernesto said.

"I have a spare apple, Ernie," Yvette chipped in.

"And I have one of Mom's super brownies," Tessie added.

"I think I'll come here to eat more often," Ernesto remarked.

CHAPTER THREE

"I don't have anything to share with you, Ernie," Naomi said. "I've eaten everything in my bag. But if you come here regularly, I'll be prepared."

"So, Naomi," Ernesto asked, "you signed up for the tryouts yet?"

"Oh Ernie," Naomi groaned. "I'm not a singer."

"I've heard you sing in church," Carmen told her. "You sounded good."

"That's different," Naomi protested. "Everybody's singing in church. If you're bad, the others drown you out. Getting up in front of people in the auditorium, that's a different story."

"You need to see Ms. D'Cruz," Ernesto urged her. "Just sign up for the tryouts, Naomi." He could see Felix Martinez's face in his mind's eye. Her dad badly wanted his daughter to have her moment in the sun.

"Okay, I'll sign up," Naomi consented, "But when the lady hears me, she'll point toward the door."

"Do you have to work after school today?" Ernesto asked. He was more concerned and suspicious than ever. His conversation with Carmen about who might have sent that phony phone message had made him nervous.

"Yeah," Naomi replied. "They want me for more hours, Jimmy said. I'm getting more shifts. That's good because I make more money toward my car. Jimmy said if it wasn't against the law, he'd have me full time."

A dark cloud moved through Ernesto's mind. Did Jimmy Ancho want Naomi more because she was good for business, or did he have personal reasons? Was he falling for her? The possibility worried Ernesto. The guy had no business falling for a sixteen-year-old high school junior—if that was really happening.

"I've seen Jimmy Ancho a few times. He seems okay," Ernesto commented, fishing around for more information.

"He's wonderful," Naomi declared. "He's so much fun to work for. He's always making jokes. He has this dry sense of humor. But he's a great boss too. He's efficient. Nothing gets by him. We've always got enough supplies."

"He must like you a lot to have given you that nice raise," Ernesto remarked.

"Oh, he didn't do that!" Naomi explained. "He was surprised when I thanked him for it. He knew nothing about it. His father did that. Elia Ancho is so cute. He sits there in his fancy business suit and keeps an eye on everything. He's really sort of a character. Like a grandfather or something."

"They're originally from Mexico, aren't they?" Carmen asked. "I think you said they're from Guadalajara."

"Yeah, I think I heard that," Naomi responded. "Jimmy speaks Spanish and perfect English. His father has a slight accent."

"Is Jimmy married?" Carmen asked. Before she asked that question, she exchanged a look with Ernesto. Carmen's eyebrows went up a little. Ernesto knew

47

Carmen well enough to recognize the gesture. Carmen wanted to know whether Jimmy was married. Maybe, she thought, he just might be interested in Naomi.

"Oh no," Naomi replied. "He's never even mentioned a girlfriend. But one girl comes in sometimes and talks to him in Spanish and English. She's a pretty blonde. You can sort of tell she's got her eye on him."

"I suppose she's about his age," Carmen commented.

Naomi caught the tone in Carmen's voice. "What's the matter, Carmen? You don't seem to like Jimmy," she asked.

"Oh, I don't even know him," Carmen objected. "But I just thought maybe he had a crush on you or something. You told me he hired you real fast out of a bunch of applicants. So I figured maybe he liked what he saw."

Naomi laughed. "Carmen, I'm sixteen years old. I'm a junior in high school. Jimmy Ancho is a businessman, twenty-five years old or something. What would he want with a kid like me? I mean, come on, Carmen. I heard him and that blonde girl talking about hanging out at some hot club downtown. They were talking about new local beer brewers and how some of the beer tastes like caramel or something. I can't even go in a place that sells liquor. What would he want with me? You think he'd be excited about hanging out with me at the pizzeria and drinking soda? It'll be like me going out with a middle-schooler boy."

Yvette and Tessie laughed, along with Naomi.

The conversation turned to other things, and then the lunch period was over.

Ernesto headed for the first of his afternoon classes. "Be sure and sign up for the tryouts," Ernesto urged Naomi. He felt a little assured that Jimmy Ancho had no designs on Naomi. Still, Ernesto resolved to deliver and pick up Naomi every time she worked.

At the end of school that day, Ernesto waited for Naomi in the Chavez parking lot. He was anxious to see her and find out how she'd done for Ms. D'Cruz. When anybody signed up for the tryouts, Ms. D'Cruz put them through a short preliminary audition. If they were very poor, she discouraged them from signing up for the formal auditions. Ernesto had read the speaking part of Cesar Chavez right after his first class. The teacher seemed very impressed.

"You have a fine, strong baritone, Ernesto," Ms. D'Cruz said. "I'm very happy that you're trying out for the role. I think you have an excellent chance."

Ernesto knew that Naomi was scheduled to try out at a later time. Ms. D'Cruz insisted on seeing the auditioners one at a time. This way, she could be honest in her opinion without embarrassing them in front of others. So Ernesto waited for Naomi in the parking lot. He was worried that Ms. D'Cruz might not let Naomi go on to the formal tryouts. Did the teacher tell Naomi that her voice just didn't measure up? Did she suggest that Naomi should skip the tryouts?

In a short while, Naomi came along with her backpack. She looked like she was dragging. She didn't look very happy. Ernesto's spirits sank at the sight of her. Felix Martinez had never asked Ernesto for a favor. When the father made his request, Ernesto was eager to accommodate him. Mr. Martinez wanted his daughter to have her moment in the spotlight. He was counting on Ernesto to help make it happen.

"Hey Naomi," Ernesto greeted her carefully. He didn't want to ask her about her meeting with Ms. D'Cruz. If it was a big flop, Naomi would be embarrassed. Ernesto didn't want to force her into admitting what happened. He thought he wouldn't even bring the subject up. "So, how was your day?" he asked.

"I was doing okay until I went to see Ms. D'Cruz," Naomi replied sourly.

Ernesto thought he heard his heart drop with a thump. "She asked me to sing for her," Naomi went on. "If I was too off the mark, she said, she wouldn't want me to do the tryouts. I sang for her in my miserable little voice, and I thought I was off the hook."

"And . . . ?" Ernesto asked, hardly able to control himself.

"Lucky me!" Naomi replied sarcastically. "She actually liked me. Now she's all excited about my chances of playing Dolores Huerta. The lady must be crazy."

A big grin broke out on Ernesto's face. "Naomi, don't put yourself down," he told her. "You have a nice voice. Ms. D'Cruz is no dummy. If she thinks you're good, you are."

"Ernie, I don't *want* to be in that thing," Naomi groaned.

"Naomi, it won't be that hard," Ernesto insisted. "Anyway, maybe you won't make the tryouts. Mira Nuñez is trying out for Dolores, and she's pretty good. I'm told she was in the school musical last year, *West Side Story*. She was Maria. So she must be good. So cheer up, Naomi. You probably won't get the part." Deep in his heart, he believed she would get it.

"Oh Ernie," Naomi complained, "with my luck I'll get it. Then I'll be stuck doing it." She seemed so depressed over the possibility that Ernesto decided he had to bring out the big guns.

"Naomi, listen," he ordered her. "I wasn't going to tell you this. And please don't tell your father that I did tell you. *He* really wants you to be in the Chavez celebration. He sort of mentioned that to me. He asked me to talk you into the tryouts. It would make him so happy to see you up there on the stage. He said some wonderful things about you. He told me all about how the family is healed because you took a chance on this party. He said he wanted everybody to know how special you are."

Naomi stared wide-eyed at Ernesto. "Ohhh!" she intoned. "So that's why you've been pushing this, Ernie. I thought it was funny that you were so determined I try out."

"Naomi," Ernesto started explaining himself fast. "The other day I ran into your father at Hortencia's. You have no idea how grateful he is to you for what you did, bringing Orlando and Manny home. He just said so many beautiful things about you. The guy was almost blubbering. He said you were so brave to bring the boys down. He said it took a lot of nerve to get Orlando to apologize and reach out to his father. He knows you were the brains and the courage behind that big birthday party that healed the family. He said having his boys back is like having a big stone lifted from his chest. He sees it's all because of you. He loves you so much, Naomi."

Naomi looked at Ernesto for a long moment without saying anything. Then she shook her head no and moaned, "Awwww!"

"No! Honest, Naomi!" Ernesto protested. "Your father said you were the family treasure. Now he said he wants you to have big moment on stage playing Dolores Huerta. He wants to be there when everybody starts cheering and stuff."

"Oh Ernie," Naomi gasped, unbelievingly. "Did Dad really say all that? Now you've done it. I was going to deliberately screw up in the audition. Now I'd feel like a rat doing that." Naomi looked at Ernesto with her amazing violet eyes.

"Yeah," Ernesto went on, feeling as though he had her persuaded. "It's finally sunk into his heart. He appreciates what you went through to get that family together again. He knows the risk you took. He said nobody else in the family woulda gone through all that. But you did, You healed the bitterness and made the family whole again."

Naomi wiped a tear from her eye with the back of her hand. "Okay," she groaned. "I'll give it my best shot. If Ms. D'Cruz is dumb enough to let me play Dolores Huerta, then I'll go for it. I know having the boys back has meant the world to Dad. But I didn't think I realized that he knew what I went through to make it happen. You were with me through it all, Ernie, and I was scared. I couldn't believe until the very end that Orlando would apologize and extend his hand to Dad."

Naomi reflected on that awful moment when Mr. Martinez did not take his son's hand. "Oh, Ernie, when Orlando reached out his hand to Dad, and Dad didn't take it right away. . . My heart almost stopped. Mom reached over and squeezed my hand so hard, I thought she'd break it. Then Dad jumped up and hugged Orlando and Manny. I just about died of joy."

"Big chance you took, babe," Ernesto told her. "Your Dad knows it. And he loves you for it."

They got into Ernesto's Volvo, and he drove her to work. As they drove down Washington Street, Ernesto noticed Clay parked in front of the pizzeria. Mira Nuñez was in the front seat with him. Their arms were around each other, and they were kissing.

"Naomi!" Ernesto pointed. "Look at them! Look at the action in the front seat of that Mustang!"

"Oh my gosh!" Naomi gasped. "They're all over each other. Oh Ernie, is that wonderful or what? He's over me. That talk you gave him worked. He's given up on me. Now he's going all out for Mira. I am so done with Clay. And now maybe he's done with me. This is wonderful. Ernie, my whole life is turning magical. I got the best boyfriend in the world and a great job. My brothers are home, and now my creepy exboyfriend has forgotten me! Life is good!"

Ernesto pulled into the parking lot of Chill Out. "Remember Naomi," he reminded her, "I'll be here to pick you up. I'll be here early."

"Ernie, I feel so bad putting you out every night," Naomi said.

"Babe," he assured her, "I'm just getting off my shift at the pizzeria anyway.

Bashar, my boss, has been moving my hours around lately. And he's giving me an extra shift once in a while. But I told him I have leave in time to pick you up. That's fine with him. So it's no trouble at all. Besides, every extra minute I can spend with you, Naomi—hey I love it. But don't forget. Stay in Chill Out until you see me. Don't be waiting in the dark, okay?"

Naomi giggled. "Ernie, you sound just like Daddy."

"Oh brother," Ernesto groaned. "I've been spending too much time with your father. It was bound to happen!"

Naomi leaned over to give Ernesto a kiss. Then she hurried in to work.

CHAPTER FOUR

Naomi Martinez had been working at Chill Out for about an hour. Then Carmen Ibarra and her boyfriend, Paul Morales, came in. Paul was eighteen, already finished with high school, and enrolled in college. He was also manager at a computer store. He and Carmen had grown very close. Naomi figured Carmen was in love with Paul.

Paul Morales was a tough young man who took no guff from anybody. Naomi had shared her concerns with Carmen about who might have sent Ernesto that phony message. Later, Carmen told Paul. Now Paul intended to have a look of his own. Naomi was touched that Carmen cared so much about her safety. She was even more impressed that Paul took it to heart.

Still, Naomi wasn't sure she wanted this much attention. Ernesto was already so anxious about her security that he picked her up every night. And her brother Orlando was worrying about the guys who came into Chill Out to ogle Naomi. Naomi felt a little suffocated by all the attention.

"I think I'll have the butterscotch with lotsa nuts on the top," Paul ordered.

Carmen nodded, "Me too."

Paul glanced around the place. Then he asked Carmen in a low voice, "Is that the dude over there? Is that Jimmy Ancho?"

"That's him," Carmen said in a whisper. They sounded as though they had already convicted Jimmy of bad intentions toward Naomi.

"He looks kinda sleazy," Paul remarked scornfully.

"Paul," Naomi groaned. "He's *not* sleazy. He's a perfect gentleman."

"I don't like those shifty eyes," Paul commented. "Notice how his eyes dart around like a lizard's looking for bugs to eat."

Naomi put out two frozen butterscotch yogurts with double toppings of pecans. Naomi asked Carmen, "Is Paul always like this?"

Carmen giggled. "Yes."

Carmen and Paul took a table in the middle of Chill Out. Naomi noticed that Paul frequently looked at Jimmy. Before long, Jimmy's silver-haired father, Elia, came in to take his favorite table. He seemed out of place here in his fancy suit. Naomi thought he should be dining at a swanky hotel downtown or somewhere like that.

When Carmen and Paul finished their yogurts, they came to the counter. "Who's the old dude?" Paul asked. "He's looking around like he owns the place."

"He does," Naomi replied, "in a way. That's Jimmy's dad, Elia Ancho. He's really sweet. He's the one gave me that big raise. He likes to keep his eye on the business."

"He likes to keep his eye on you too, girl," Paul declared grimly. "He's really staring at you."

"Oh Paul," Naomi objected, "don't be ridiculous. He's old enough to be my grandfather. He's a nice, dignified older man."

"I don't care," Paul insisted. "Some dudes are never too old to look at hot chicks."

Naomi looked at Carmen and inquired, "Has this guy met many people he actually trusts and likes?"

Paul threw his arm around Carmen's shoulders and declared with a sly grin. "This babe here. I trust her, and I more than like her. But other than that, I don't trust too many people."

Paul noticed the curious look on Naomi's face. She didn't know what to make of him. He continued. "I've seen too much of the dark side of life, Naomi. Foster homes where there's people swearing they're in it for love of the kids. Then you get there, and you're just a monthly check to them. I've lived too long on the shady side of the street to have many illusions. Most people are on the make or the take. It's a dangerous world."

Carmen smiled at Naomi and explained, "Paul's in kind of a bad mood. One of the employees down at the computer store was helping himself to stuff. Paul caught him and had to blow the whistle. It was a bad scene."

"Just make sure Ernie has your back, Naomi," Paul advised. "The woods are full of wolves. Some of them are very hungry, and they got big teeth."

Naomi knew Carmen was close to loving Paul Morales. Paul had many good qualities, but Naomi would not have wanted a boyfriend like that. His personality was too dark. It wasn't his fault. He lost his mother early, and his dad was never there. He was bounced around from one foster home to another. The same thing happened to his brother, David, who was now an inmate at the state prison, doing time for burglary. Paul visited David faithfully and was planning for when he got out. Paul intended to provide a home and help his brother get back on track when his time was served. Naomi really respected Paul Morales for that. He wouldn't turn his back on someone he loved. If Carmen and Paul turned out to be partners, Naomi knew he'd be as faithful to her and their family. That'd be good.

Near the end of Naomi's shift, no other customers were in Chill Out. Even Jimmy Ancho had left for the night. But Elia Ancho continued to sit at his table, looking up from time to time. Two boys she'd never seen before came in. She didn't think they were students at Cesar Chavez High School.

"Chocolate with cherries on the top, doll face," one of the boys ordered, smiling at Naomi.

"I want a vanilla yogurt with coconut flakes, baby," the other boy said.

Naomi was glad Sherry Carranza was at the counter too. The boys seemed too brazen. But they took their frozen yogurts and went to a booth without making further comments. Naomi breathed a sigh of relief. She glanced at Mr. Ancho and asked Sherry, "Does Mr. Ancho have a wife?"

"No, he's a widower," Sherry replied. "He lost his wife about a year ago."

"Oh, that's sad," Naomi responded. "He seems so lonely. It's sad that he sits around a yogurt shop for hours on end like this. It's like he's depressed or something."

Naomi assumed that Mr. Ancho and his wife had been married for many years and that she had become his everything. Losing a long-time soul mate was probably harder on a man than a woman. Women tend to have a bigger support system of friends. Naomi felt really sorry for the man. "Did Jimmy's mother die suddenly," Naomi asked. "Or was she sick a long time?"

"Oh, Mr. Ancho's wife wasn't Jimmy's mother," Sherry explained. "Mr. Ancho and Jimmy's mother were divorced a long time ago. Mr. Ancho had just married his second wife a year ago. She was much younger than him. And he adored her. I never really saw her. From her picture, she looked so beautiful. They had a huge wedding in the Caribbean. Then they went on a honeymoon cruise, and Mrs. Ancho apparently fell overboard. It was so tragic. They never even found her body. A person hates to think of it. But she disappeared in warm water where there are . . . you know . . . sharks. . ."

"Oh my gosh!" Naomi gasped. "What a horrible thing to have happened. No wonder the poor man is so sad."

The two boys who had come in earlier finished their yogurts and now came to the counter where Naomi stood.

"Hey baby," one of them said, "when do you get off work?"

"I hope you enjoyed your yogurts and do come again," Naomi replied politely.

"We have a special on Friday. Buy one frozen yogurt and get the second one at half price."

"That wasn't the question, sweet thing," the boy persisted. "My name is Mike Baca. What's yours?"

The other boy laughed. "She's as cold as the yogurt, dude," he remarked, turning to go.

But Mike Baca wasn't ready to go.

"Have a nice night," Naomi said.

"I would if you went out with me, honey," Mike Baca responded. The boy was tall with shaggy hair. He wasn't bad looking. But he looked like a dropout, maybe even a gang wannabe.

Suddenly Mr. Ancho was up from the table and beside Mike Baca. "I want you to leave this place at once," he told the boy sharply. "We do not permit customers to harass our employees."

"Who're you, old man?" Mike Baca snapped, a sneer on his lips. "Did you escape from the nursing home?"

Rage glowed in Mr. Ancho's eyes. The second boy backed off fast and was heading for the door. The older man looked about sixty, but he was tall and well built. He looked as though he could put up quite a fight.

"It's all right, Mr. Ancho," Naomi intervened. "This boy is leaving right now. It's all right. Everything's under control."

"No, it's not all right," Mr. Ancho said. "This thug was harassing you, and I will not let that stand." Mr. Ancho reached out and grabbed the boy by the neck, shouting in his face, "You will never come into this establishment again, do you hear me? Never!"

"Oh my gosh," Sherry Carranza gasped.

Mike Baca's eyes were bulging, and he was having trouble breathing. Mr. Ancho's hands tightened around his throat. The second boy was at the door, but he saw what was happening. "Somebody call nine-one-one!" he screamed. "I don' got my cell! He's killin' Mike!"

At that moment Mr. Ancho thrust Mike Baca away from him. The boy fell on the floor, gasping for breath. He scrambled to his feet and ran frantically to the door. He vanished into the darkness with his friend.

Naomi was drenched in cold perspiration. Sherry looked ashen.

"Are you all right?" Mr. Ancho asked Naomi. "I'm very sorry that thug bothered you. I'm sure it will never happen again. I put the fear of the Lord in him. Vermin like him must be dealt with forthrightly. I would imagine he's still running out there." A faint smile came to the man's face.

Naomi didn't know what to say. She felt she had been in no danger from Mike Baca or his friend. They were just silly young punks. Naomi could have dealt with them with no problem. She dealt with a lot worse at school. Mr. Ancho's reaction horrified her.

"I'm all right," Naomi finally found the voice to say. "I'm fine."

Mr. Ancho glanced at the expensive watch on his wrist. "Well, we'll be closing down soon. I believe I'll be going." He looked right into Naomi's eyes and stated, "You shouldn't have to deal with scum like that. You are a most lovely girl. But that does not mean you may be denied the respect that you deserve. Do you have a ride home? If not I—"

"No, it's all right," Naomi replied quickly. "Someone's picking me up. Thank you."

"Because my BMW is parked right out there," Mr. Ancho offered. "And I would be happy to take you home. Anytime you need a ride, just let me know. It would be my pleasure."

"Thank you," Naomi said, pushing the words through her dry mouth. She breathed a deep sigh of relief when Mr. Ancho went out the door. She was happy to hear the sound of his engine turning over.

Naomi looked at Sherry. "Has he ever done anything like that before?" she asked. "I was so scared. I was terrified. I couldn't believe what I was seeing. I almost fainted.

I thought he was going to strangle that kid. The kid's eyes were bulging out. Oh my gosh, I thought he was going to murder that boy."

"I've never seen him go that far," Sherry answered. "He's yelled at customers for paying too much attention to the girls at the counter, but nothing violent. He's erratic. We had a girl in here before, Josie. She was real hot. She wore tight clothes, and some of the young guys hit on her. Mr. Ancho got angry at them and chased them out, but he never actually attacked somebody. I was about to call nine-one-one like that other kid was yelling. I figured it would cost me my job, but I couldn't let him kill the kid."

"Oh man," Naomi gasped, leaning on the counter. "I'm still shaking." Naomi looked at Sherry. "He needs help. That's not normal, Sherry. You know it's not normal."

"I guess he's still grieving for Alexa," Sherry said. "That was his wife's name.

I don't know the circumstances about how she died on that cruise ship. But I heard rumors that some guys onboard were a little drunk, and they were sorta hitting on her. Maybe he blamed them for her going over or something."

Sherry shrugged her shoulders. "Jimmy told me his dad was so hysterical when he lost Alexa like that. He had to be taken to the hospital for a long time. It was so awful to lose her like that. The man had a beautiful young bride one minute, and then she's dead somewhere in the water. Not even a body to bury."

"Sherry, I love this job and the money is good," Naomi admitted. "But if stuff like this is gonna happen, I can't take it. I think this is the most horrible thing I ever saw. I've seen gang fights, but this was worse. I really thought he would choke that kid to death."

"I'll call Jimmy tonight and tell him what happened," Sherry promised. "Maybe Jimmy can get his father into a hospital, and he can be evaluated. He might need meds, you know. He's got depression and maybe other issues too. Maybe things just got the best of him tonight. But otherwise, you couldn't want a nicer man."

Sherry gave Naomi a hug and said, "I think I hear your boyfriend out there. I hear that 'Volvo' sound. You go and get a good night's sleep, honey. I'll shut things down here."

Naomi grabbed her purse and hurried out the door. Sherry locked the door behind her. Naomi was never so glad to be out of anyplace as she was to escape Chill Out. She saw the Volvo and ran toward it. Ernesto was out of the car, leaning on the fender. He immediately recognized her distress. "What's the matter, babe?" he asked. "You look like you've seen a ghost or something!"

Naomi ran into Ernesto's arms, and he held her for several seconds. "Babe, you're shaking like you got chills and fever. What happened? What's the matter?"

"I'm okay," Naomi assured him. "I'm okay now. But oh, Ernie, what a night!" She got into the passenger side of the car. She lay her head back against the head rest, closing her eyes.

"Oh Ernie," she spoke with her eyes closed, "this kid came in Chill Out. He was kinda hitting on me, but nothing serious. I could handle it easy. It was nothing. I was real cool about it, and everything was fine. But then Elia Ancho came running over like a madman and he grabbed the kid by the throat!"

"*What?*" Ernesto gasped.

"Yeah, the place was empty except for Sherry and me and this kid and his friend," she explained, "and Mr. Ancho. Ernie, he was choking the kid! The kid's eyes were bulging out, and he couldn't breathe. The kid's friend was screaming that we should call nine-one-one. Sherry almost did, but then Mr. Ancho let the kid go. The kid dropped to the floor. But he got up real quick and went tearing out the door, running for his life! Oh Ernie, it was so horrible. Mr. Ancho was like insane!"

"Babe, you gotta quit that job right now," Ernesto advised. "You can't go back there."

"No, it's okay," Naomi objected. "Sherry is gonna call his son, Jimmy. She's calling him tonight, and they'll get Mr. Ancho into the hospital. He needs medication for depression or something. Sherry told me something tonight about Mr. Ancho."

Ernesto was waiting for traffic to pull out of the lot. "What's that?" he asked, as he hit the gas pedal.

"He'd just married a second wife about a year ago," Naomi explained. "They were on their honeymoon cruise when she fell overboard. She was never found. There were sharks in the water there."

Ernesto glanced at her and grimaced. But her eyes were still closed.

"Ever since then," she went on, "Mr. Ancho has been kinda off the wall. Sherry thinks Jimmy will get him into therapy immediately."

Naomi took a long, deep breath and exhaled. She finally had stopped shaking. "I'm okay now, Ernie. But I've never seen anything like that before. I've seen kids fighting on the street. But this man had murder in his eyes. It was like he wasn't going to quit until the kid stopped breathing. This adult man had been sitting quietly at the table doing a crossword puzzle from the newspaper. All of a sudden he's crazy like that. It was . . . so bad."

"You guys should have called nine-one-one," Ernesto said. "He shouldn't even be on the street driving a car if he's that nuts. Naomi, I hate to think of you going back to work there. I really do. I don't care if the guy's wife fell overboard or whatever. He must be a nut case to have acted like he did tonight."

He drove silently for a few seconds, thinking. "It would've been different," Ernesto commented, "if the kid was grabbing you or something. Or even if he was just threatening you with harm. Then I'd say the guy was just coming to your defense. But if the kid was just horsing around . . ."

"Ernie," Naomi pleaded. "Please don't mention this to my dad. He would just totally freak out. He'd demand I quit the job. And I don't want to quit. I love the job, and the money is so good. I know Jimmy'll take care of the situation. The minute Jimmy hears from Sherry, he'll get his father into a clinic or something. I doubt that we'll ever see Mr. Ancho near Chill Out again. Okay?"

Ernesto didn't respond right away. She went on. "I don't want to lose such a great job when nothing like this will ever happen again. I'd kick myself from one end of the *barrio* to the other if I quit the job. Then Mr. Ancho never comes to the place again."

"The next time you go to work, I'll get someone to cover my shift at the pizzeria. I'll just eat one yogurt after another so I can keep my eye on you."

That remark broke the tension. Naomi started to giggle, then laugh. She pictured poor Ernesto sitting there, stuffing himself with frozen yogurt until he was so sick. In her mind's eye, he falls on the floor and has to be carried out. "Ernie, you're such a sweet guy, I'm not going to let you lose pay. This'll probably never happen again." Naomi chuckled. "But you'd do that for me wouldn't you?"

"I'd do anything to keep you safe, babe," Ernesto said very seriously.

"Well," Naomi said, "I don't work again until Wednesday. By then, Jimmy'll have things straightened out."

Then Naomi took a long look at Ernie. "What did I ever do to deserve you?" she asked, still snickering. "When we first met, you'd just come back from Los Angeles. I was hooked up with Clay Aguirre. Any other guy would have taken me for one stupid chick. I was taking all that rudeness Clay was dishing out. Any other guy would have just written me off as a lost cause. But you hung in there patiently, waiting for me to come to my senses. You saw me falling, babe, and you were there to catch me. I've got to be the luckiest girl in the world."

"I'm the lucky one," Ernesto objected. "In the beginning I thought I didn't have a chance. But even if I wasn't ever gonna get a date with you, I wanted to help you see what Clay was like. A girl can't be happy with a guy like him. I see him now with Mira, and I feel sorry for her. I'm glad Clay is with her, but that's for a selfish reason. Better her than you. But I feel sorry for her anyway."

Ernesto turned down Bluebird Street and parked in the Martinez driveway. "I'm coming in for a few minutes. Okay, Naomi?" he asked. "I want to say hello to Brutus and your folks. It seems kinda rude to just let you out of the car and go home."

"You won't say anything about what happened?" Naomi said.

"I won't," Ernesto promised, but he wanted to.

When Naomi and Ernesto walked in, Felix Martinez was sitting in his favorite

79

chair, talking on the phone. "What's it like over there?" he was asking, a smile on his face. "Crazy gamblers walkin' around in a daze 'cause they lost their shirts at the craps tables?"

Mr. Martinez laughed and put the phone aside for a minute. "I'm talkin' to Orlando. The boys are over in Vegas with the Perez band. They got a big gig. They're opening for some big shot."

He returned to the phone, "Poor stiffs. Don't they get it? The house always wins. Yeah. . . . When you guys go on? I'll be thinking of you. Hey, Orlando, say 'hi' to Manny. Tell him his hair looks really good now that it's longer. Naomi, she just come in now with Ernie. Brutus is goin' nuts. He's jumpin' on all the furniture."

He laughed again. "See you in two weeks, boy. Love ya. I told your mom no butterfinger squash and Rosemary's cheese this time. It's *carne asada* all the way. Yeah!"

Naomi marveled again at the difference in her father's personality since her brothers were reconciled. Felix Martinez had a new lease on life. The whole family had a new lease on life.

"So Naomi, how did it go over at Chill Out?" Dad asked.

"Okay Dad," Naomi replied. "We were busy."

"Me and Naomi signed up for the tryouts for the Chavez birthday celebration, Mr. Martinez," Ernesto mentioned.

"Good, good!" Naomi's father responded. He sat there and took a long look at his daughter. "You know what, sweetheart," he told her. "I'm glad me and Linda didn't call it a day after Zack was born. I'm glad we went for one more kid. Boy, oh boy, did we hit the jackpot!"

Naomi walked over to her father's chair and kissed him on the top of the head. He had the same thick, curly, blue-black hair that his sons had, but his was frosted with silver tips. A lot of men his age were balding, but he looked as though he'd never lose his hair.

CHAPTER FIVE

Before long, the day of the formal auditions was on hand. It was the start of the school week.

Naomi had seen Angelina D'Cruz around the Chavez campus since her freshman year. But they never met. Ms. D'Cruz was about forty. She had planned to be an operatic singer but was happy teaching music to high schoolers.

When Naomi and Ernesto went in for the audition in the Chavez auditorium, about two dozen students were waiting their turn. Ms. D'Cruz and a young teacher from the community college would do the selections.

Five young men were auditioning for the speaking role of Cesar Chavez.

"We're looking for good strong voices," Ms. D'Cruz explained. "We're also looking for passion. We want the student who plays Cesar Chavez to show the dedication that Chavez himself had for his cause. The *causa* he fought for was his whole life. This is the kind of spirit the winning student will show."

To prepare for his audition, Ernesto Sandoval had done a lot of research on Cesar Chavez. He not only memorized several speeches, but he delved deeply into what the man was fighting for. When Chavez started to unionize the grape pickers in Delano, California, their average annual wage was only $1,500 a year. At the time, the poverty level for a family in the United States was $3,000. Chavez struggled, marched, and fasted for the farmworkers. He literally gave his life to help them. In the fields, there were often no toilets. Farmworkers had to pay for drinking water. Dangerous pesticides were sprayed on them as they harvested the crops. Ernesto tried to absorb all this and to let it come out in his audition.

A senior and a junior auditioned first, and Ernesto thought they were good. He was nervous when he stepped up to speak. Ms. D'Cruz allowed the students to bring props for their audition, and Ernesto brought the union flag. He held up the flag showing the sacred Aztec bird—the eagle—drawn in straight lines. The black eagle was drawn on a white circle. The rest of the flag was red. "The black eagle," Ernesto intoned, "stands for our people's troubles as they fight for justice. The white stands for hope. The red symbolizes the struggle for *la causa. ¡Viva la causa!*"

Ernesto used the poignant speech Cesar Chavez often gave about his own background. Ernesto described the Chavez family's drive west to California in an old Studebaker. At the migrant camp, they were told that the rundown shacks rented for two dollars a night. But the family didn't have the two dollars. So they slept in the

Studebaker. The next day the whole family got a job picking grapes. They were told they would be paid at the end of the week. But when that time came to be paid, they were not given the promised wages. They could do nothing. They had to take whatever was done to them. They had no power. Ernesto really threw his heart and soul into the audition. He felt good about how he'd done.

When Ernesto finished, Ms. D'Cruz was beaming. She leaned over in animated conversation with the teacher from the community college.

Ernesto rejoined the audience to hear the six girls try out for the role of Dolores Huerta. Dolores Huerta had not been a singer. But for this celebration they had given her a song to express her devotion to *la causa*.

All of the girls trying out were attractive. Naomi Martinez thought she didn't have much of a chance. She felt bad now that Ernesto had told her how much her father wanted her to be in the program. Because of her father, Naomi had been working with Orlando and Manny. She tried to do her very best. Before she knew about her father's wishes, Naomi had decided she would not put her heart into the effort.

When Naomi was younger, she and her brothers had the little garage band. She had a nice, strong soprano, and she would belt out the Mexican ballads impressively. She and Orlando and Manny dreamed of the three of them hitting the big time one day. But when Orlando and Manny moved away, Naomi forgot all about singing. Now, suddenly, she was standing before Ms. D'Cruz and the community college teacher. She was doing her audition.

A music student from the college played the piano as Naomi sang.

The struggle is not for me,
The struggle is for them,
Por los niños, for the children,
The children of the land,

The children in the fields,
Por los niños, for the children.
We are today, they are tomorrow,
We fight to heal their pain,
Their sorrow falls like rain,
Por los niños, por los niños . . .

When she finished, Naomi hurried off stage, not looking at the judges. She saw Ms. D'Cruz and the college teacher putting their heads together later. When all the auditions were over, Ms. D'Cruz told everyone that the winners would be announced at the end of the school day on Friday.

As Naomi and Ernesto walked out together, Naomi declared, "You aced it, Ernie. You sounded great. Using that beautiful union flag was icing on the cake. But I think they'll get somebody else to be Dolores. Maybe that girl, Nancy. She was good."

"I'm not counting you out, babe," Ernesto told her. "That song you sang shook me to my soul."

"Well, we'll see," Naomi said. "When I was in middle school, I thought maybe I'd be a singer someday. I had crushes on a bunch of singers. My room was papered with pop star posters. Now I've gotten rid of all of them, and my walls are covered with pandas."

"I always wanted to be a teacher, like Dad," Ernesto responded. "He does so much good. I planned to go to the community college where it's cheaper, then transfer to State and get my teaching credential. Now I'm not so sure. I think I might want something else."

Naomi looked at Ernesto. "What do you want now, babe?"

"Maybe law school," Ernesto replied.

"Like your Uncle Arturo," Naomi remarked. "But lawyers are dealing with squabbling people all the time . . ."

"Maybe after law school . . . politics," Ernesto went on.

"Politics?" Naomi repeated. "Wow, are you serious?"

"Yeah," Ernesto said emphatically, "our country needs more Hispanics in politics. I mean, helping with Emilio Ibarra's campaign, that sorta got me going, Naomi. Mr. Ibarra has already done some good things to help people. Like he's revived the scholarship program for deserving kids who couldn't otherwise afford college. He's helped the veterans. He's doing good stuff, Naomi. He's working for people. I like that idea."

"Yeah, you're right," Naomi agreed.

"When you get up into the federal level into Congress," Ernesto went on, "you can make things happen. I know everybody likes to say how the government is filled with crooks, but it doesn't have to be that way. Some of the people in government are crooks, but some of them are heroes too."

"You'd be one of the heroes, Ernie," Naomi assured him. "You're already my hero."

"Babe, you're my hero," Ernesto responded. "Look what you did for your family. A lot of times when I dropped you off at that house on Bluebird Street, I thought, 'How does she stay sane with all that going on?' But you did, and you healed your family."

He couldn't help smiling at her. He loved her so much. "So what about your dreams? What do you want to do, Naomi?"

"I have no idea," she answered. "I'm still thinking. One day I want to be a teacher, and the next day maybe a nurse or a doctor. Sometimes I'd like to fly a plane, and the next day I'd like to be a vet and work with animals. Once I even thought I'd join Cirque du Soleil. The only thing I'm sure about my future, Ernie, is that I want you to be a part of it. I want you to be there with me. I can't imagine a future without you."

Ernesto turned and grabbed her, holding her close. "That's good that you feel that way, babe, 'cause I'm never letting go of you."

On Wednesday, Naomi was scheduled to work at Chill Out. Usually she looked forward to going to work. She knew the job now inside and out, and seeing all the regular customers was fun. She'd get the frozen peppermint yogurt for the two elderly ladies with blue hair. She'd get the orange yogurt with the candied orange slices on top for the family with redheaded boys. But this Wednesday, Naomi was uneasy. She was afraid that, eventually, Elia Ancho would come in to sit at his regular table, staring at her.

Naomi had tried calling Sherry Carranza to find out what was going on. But Sherry was always out. Now, as Naomi walked into Chill Out, Sherry greeted her with a cheerful thumbs-up. Jimmy Ancho was there, filling the topping containers. When he saw Naomi he hailed her. "Naomi, come into the back room for a minute."

Naomi wasn't sure what to expect. Was Jimmy going to scold her. Perhaps she was being too nice to the customers. Did he think she was inviting the unwanted attention that caused the trouble?

When Naomi went into the back room, Jimmy closed the door, giving them privacy. "Naomi," he said in a very serious voice. "I'm really sorry about what happened the other night. It must have been very frightening for you. I blame myself because I've been seeing signs of Dad's mental deterioration for several weeks. I just ignored it. I kept telling myself he'd snap out of it. You know, my parents divorced several years ago, and it was a bitter experience for my father. Then, when he remarried, his bride died under tragic circumstances. It was all too much for him."

Naomi stood there in silence. She was hoping that Jimmy would tell her that his father was under treatment and would not be returning.

"Father's behavior has been erratic since he and Mom divorced," Jimmy explained. "When he met this beautiful young woman and married her after a month, we were all stunned. That just wasn't like my dad. I think he was desperately trying to fill his loneliness. My father and Alexa had this large wedding, and they were on their honeymoon cruise when she fell overboard. It was so devastating for him. He was deeply in love with Alexa, and her death, well, unhinged him."

Naomi felt as if Jimmy was trying to get around to saying something difficult. "Unfortunately, Naomi," Jimmy said finally, "you bear a striking resemblance to Alexa. She was so beautiful. She had the same luxuriant curly hair, her eyes . . . When my father saw you, he became transfixed. I didn't realize it, but he transferred his grief over losing Alexa into an obsession to protect you. In some strange way, by defending you against those boys who were flirting with you, he was saving Alexa."

Jimmy's eyes were averted from Naomi's. He couldn't look her in the eye as he said what he had to say. "But," he continued, "that having been said, you needn't worry about his behavior anymore. We own a lot of property in Guadalajara. Father has gone down there to stay with my sisters. They'll be looking after him and making sure he takes his medication. You won't be seeing him around here anymore."

"So," Jimmy concluded, smiling wryly, "we can all get on with the important business of serving frozen yogurt without this sad distraction. I'm hoping the warm family environment down with my sisters will restore Father's health in time. I'm very sorry you had to go through that experience, Naomi. Thank you for having the courage to continue to work here."

Naomi didn't know what to say for a few moments. "Thank you so much for sharing all this," she finally responded. She felt sorry for the young man. This experience had to be terribly difficult for Jimmy Ancho too. "I love working here. Everybody's wonderful, and I hope your dad gets better."

Jimmy Ancho smiled. "Thank you, Naomi. I hoped you'd understand," he said. "I believed you would because you're a remarkable young woman."

Naomi was thrilled that the problem with Elia Ancho had been resolved. She put on her snowman T-shirt, went outside, and got behind the counter. The customers started coming in, and Naomi all but forgot the terrible incident.

They were very busy at Chill Out for about two hours. Then the customer traffic thinned out. Sherry looked at Naomi and summoned her over by flexing her pointing finger. "Come here," the gesture said. The look on Sherry's face said, "I have something to show you."

With Naomi at her side, Sherry dug into her purse and pulled out the wedding photo of Elia and Alexa Ancho. "Here's his second wife, the girl who drowned. See why he went nuts about you, Naomi?" she asked.

Naomi stared at the strikingly beautiful girl in the photo. "She looks so young,"

Naomi remarked. "She must have been much, much younger than him."

"She was only nineteen," Sherry said.

"Nineteen!" Naomi gasped. "And he's like sixty! She was only a couple years older than me."

"Yeah, they met at a fitness spa," Sherry explained. "Mr. Ancho was told by his doctor to get more exercise, and Alexa worked there. He showered her with amazing gifts. Alexa was still a senior in high school when they met. She got married to him a week after her high school graduation. He bought her a sports car as a wedding gift. It was really weird."

"Wow!" Naomi exclaimed. "There must have been like forty years between them. That is so amazing. I can't imagine any girl marrying a man old enough to be her grandfather."

"Well, he's very rich," Sherry said. "That counts for a lot with some chicks. What's that old saying? I'd rather be a rich man's trophy than a poor man's slave—or something like that. But it didn't turn out so good for her. She wasn't rich for long."

Naomi remembered the text message Ernesto got some nights ago. The message was that Naomi wouldn't need a ride home. Now Naomi told Sherry what happened. "You don't think Mr. Ancho could have sent that message, do you, Sherry? He stood at the door that night, and he offered to drive me home. But I guess that's not possible because how could Mr. Ancho have gotten my boyfriend's cell number."

Sherry's eyes lit up. "I bet that's just who did send it, Naomi! Remember when you made out your application to work here? You filled in some names as references. One of them was your boyfriend, Ernesto Sandoval. You noted that he was the assistant manager at the pizzeria. I guess you thought that would carry some credibility. But his cell phone number was right there. I saw Mr. Ancho looking at your application. That's where he got your boyfriend's number."

"That's so creepy if that's what happened, Sherry," Naomi remarked. "Man I'm glad he's gone. I gotta admit, Mr. Ancho made me uncomfortable. Okay, he would sit over there at his table and stare at me. But I never dreamed he was making some sick connection between me and that poor girl who fell off the cruise ship."

"Yeah," Sherry agreed, "I hope his daughters keep him down there in Mexico for good. A guy like that shouldn't be roaming around by himself living in fantasies."

When it was about half an hour to quitting time, the door of Chill Out opened. In walked Ernesto Sandoval. "Am I too late for a frozen strawberry yogurt?" Ernesto asked. "I've just got a yearning for a frozen strawberry yogurt." He had a sheepish grin on his face.

Naomi put out the strawberry yogurt with fresh strawberries on the top. She added a dollop of whipped cream. "You're early, Ernie. I wasn't expecting you for almost thirty minutes," Naomi commented.

"Oh yeah," Ernesto replied. "Well, it was slow at the pizzeria tonight. So I asked to take off a little early, And, like I said, I just got to thinking how good a frozen strawberry yogurt would be about now. I just get these urges for things late at night."

Ernesto sat down at a table and ate his yogurt. Naomi wondered how long he had actually been out in the parking lot. Did he skip working tonight? Had he been looking around and checking things out? Had he been making sure there was no Mustang or BMW parked anywhere near the back door?

Naomi looked at Ernesto sitting there, eating his yogurt. She noticed he was looking around. He was giving special attention to the now empty table where Mr. Ancho used to sit.

Naomi gazed at Ernesto, at his warm, dark eyes, at his blue black hair, at the kindness in his face. She felt such a surge of love for him that it felt like an earthquake.

CHAPTER SIX

At the end of her shift, Naomi and Ernesto went out to the car. As they got into it, Naomi said, "We don't have to worry about Mr. Ancho anymore. Jimmy had a long talk with me. He apologized for what we had to deal with the other night when his father freaked out. He said he'd been watching him going downhill for a long time. He blamed himself for not doing something earlier. The good part is, Mr. Ancho is now down in Mexico with his daughters. They're going to see that he takes his medications. He'll be staying there until he's well."

"Beautiful," Ernesto said heartily. "I am so glad to hear that, babe. I never want to see that guy around here again. I feel sorry for whatever happened to him that sent him into a tailspin. But I just worried myself sick about you being in the middle of it."

When Ernesto brought Naomi home, he went in the Martinez house to say hello. He was surprised to find Felix Martinez in a very bad mood. Since his sons had come home, Mr. Martinez was generally in a great frame of mind. Now he was on the phone and fuming about something, as in the bad old days. He was speaking with his cousin Monte Esposito.

"Yeah, Eppy just called me, Monte," Mr. Martinez said on the phone. "Poor guy, he messed up his old truck bad on that lousy Oriole Street. You know the city put in new water pipes, and they patched up the street. Well, they did a crummy job. Thought anything was good enough for the losers on Oriole Street. And you think that bum Ibarra is gonna go to bat for those people? Not a chance. Ibarra just cares about the people livin' over on Nuthatch!"

Monte said something Naomi and Ernesto couldn't hear. "Yeah," Dad said, "Eppy said a kid was skateboarding there. He hit one of those potholes and almost busted his head. Gonna be a bad accident on Oriole or Starling. Car's gonna go out of control on that rough street and go flyin' into a kid's bedroom or something." Felix Martinez was ranting.

Ernesto exchanged a worried look with Naomi. When Mr. Martinez put down the phone, Ernesto said, "Is the city council going to consider repaving Oriole and Starling?"

"Yeah, it's on their docket," Felix Martinez sneered. "If my cousin Monte was still down there, he'd have something done right away. But Ibarra, he couldn't care less. He didn't get no campaign contributions from the poor people on Oriole and Starling. So they can just suck wind."

Mr. Martinez flopped down in his chair. "If Monte was still down there, you'd see action. But Ibarra only cares about his fat cat friends. Sure, he throws some money to the bums who live in the ravine. That's just to show what a good guy he is. Ibarra doesn't care about working people like Eppy. He just wiped out his truck on that street."

Eppy Pastro had been a friend of Felix Martinez for almost thirty years. They worked for the same construction company, and both started out doing menial jobs. Naomi's father kept taking training so he could move into heavy machinery. Eppy never felt capable enough. So he was still stuck with the menial jobs, making a low salary. Oriole Street, where Eppy lived, had older, smaller houses. Routinely, the city made improvements on streets like Nuthatch and Bluebird. But it neglected streets like Oriole and Starling.

"Mr. Martinez," Ernesto suggested, "Mr. Ibarra has open-door office hours on Thursday afternoons from four to six. Why don't you go down there? You could talk to him about the problem."

Naomi's father laughed bitterly. "You think that bum would talk to me? He knows I hate his guts. He knows how I feel about him knocking my cousin off the city council. Come on, Ernie, don't be a fool. All I'd have to do is show my face near that clown's office. He'd call the deputy sheriff on me."

"Daddy," Naomi spoke up, "I'm sure Mr. Ibarra will do the right thing. But maybe he doesn't realize how bad those streets are. Maybe he's just doesn't know it's an emergency. Ernie and me could take pictures of the busted-up paving on Oriole and Starling streets. We could use our phones. Right after school tomorrow, we could do that. We could prove to Mr. Ibarra how desperately those streets need repaving."

"You're a wonderful girl, Naomi," Dad declared. "You got a heart of gold, and I love you for that. But you're a little bit soft in the head sometimes. You don't wanna believe how bad some people are. That clown with his big mustache, he ain't interested in looking at your pictures."

"Tell you what, Mr. Martinez," Ernesto suggested. "Naomi and I'll leave school together tomorrow. We'll go right over to Oriole and Starling and get pictures. We'll meet you when you get out of work. Then the three of us can ride in my Volvo down to Emilio Ibarra's office. We can make him look at the evidence. Let's see whether he talks to us tomorrow afternoon. He said he'll talk to anybody who comes in. I swear to you, Mr. Martinez, if he gives us the runaround, I'll make a big stink. Me and some of my friends will go down to the city council meeting on Tuesday. We'll make a scene. That's a promise."

Felix Martinez stared at Ernesto. "Are you serious?" he asked.

"Yeah, I am," Ernesto asserted. "I've driven on Oriole Street since they put in the new water pipes and repaved. It was a crummy job. Even I could see that. What you're saying is true. It's an outrage. It started out just disgusting looking. Now it's dangerous. A car going a little too fast could hit one of those ruts, and there could be an awful accident."

Naomi's father turned to his daughter and commented, "Listen to this kid. He sounds like a firebrand."

Looking back at Ernesto, he told him, "Hey, you're all right, Ernie. You were a *Zapatista*. But now you figure maybe you made a mistake. Okay, Ernie, I'm onboard with you on this."

Mr. Martinez leaned forward in his chair. "I'll make you a bet, Ernie. Let's say Ibarra takes one look at me standing there and slams the door shut. If he does, you gotta buy me and Linda nice dinners. I like that new Greek restaurant that just opened up. If he talks to us, then you and Naomi can go there on me. Have yourself some *gyros*, salad, and fries. But I'm pretty sure how this thing is gonna go. Me and Linda, we're gonna be steppin' out."

When Ernesto got home after delivering Naomi, he told his parents about Felix

Martinez's newest gripe, "His buddy, Eppy, lives over on Oriole. He damaged his old truck really bad on that busted-up street. Eppy doesn't have the money to repair the truck. So I saw Naomi's father sticking a few hundred dollars in an envelope to take over there."

"That was good of Felix," Luis Sandoval remarked. "Yes, that's a legitimate gripe. Both Oriole and Starling are nightmares to drive. When I have to go on those streets, I just creep along for fear of killing my alignment or blowing a tire at least."

"Those streets have the poorest people in the *barrio*," Maria Sandoval added. "It makes me sick that they're neglected. We got new water pipes here on Wren a couple years ago. They repaved beautifully. The street felt like velvet. I think those stinkers down in city hall don't care as much about the people on Oriole and Starling."

"That's not right," Ernesto objected. "That's the way Monte Esposito operated. But I hope it's not the way Emilio Ibarra is gonna operate. Guys like Eppy have as much right to a smooth street as we do. Mr. Ibarra has open-office hours on Thursday afternoons. So me and Naomi are getting pictures with our phones. We're going down to city hall with Naomi's father to show Mr. Ibarra the conditions there."

Luis Sandoval got a half amused, half frightened look on his face. "Oh brother, Ernie!" he exclaimed. "That is going to be interesting. Emilio knows how much Felix hates him since Felix's cousin lost the city council seat. I shudder to think of those two guys coming face to face."

"That's why we're bringing Naomi along," Ernesto explained with a wry smile. "I'm hoping her father won't act up as much with her there. Besides, Mr. Ibarra knows that Naomi and his daughter, Carmen, are great friends. So that might cool him down too."

"Don't count on that happening, Ernie," Luis Sandoval warned. "When those two guys see each other, I think there will be fireworks. Just get out of the way. I've seen both of them go ballistic. If you see Emilio's mustache quivering on his lip, consider running."

"Well, Mr. Martinez has been pretty good lately," Ernesto said. "Since his sons are home, he's more pleasant to everybody. I was really surprised to find him so angry tonight."

"I think Felix Martinez is the kind of a person who kind of enjoys being angry about something," Ernesto's mother remarked. "And Emilio is a wonderful target. Felix is really close to his cousin. When he lost that job on the city council, Emilio became the devil."

"Emilio is no shrinking violet either," Dad commented. "I've seen him on the warpath, and it's not a pretty sight. You and Naomi are very brave, Ernie. More power to you."

A little later that evening, Ernesto got Carmen Ibarra on her cell phone. He told her about the three of them coming to her father's office the next day. "Mr. Martinez is really steamed about the conditions on Oriole Street," Ernesto explained. "His buddy's truck was severely damaged. He hit a pothole and something cracked. You know, they have that council meeting coming up on Tuesday. Naomi's father is sure that your dad is gonna vote against repaving Oriole and Starling. And tomorrow he's gonna really let your dad have it."

"Oh my gosh," Carmen groaned. "Felix Martinez is actually coming to Dad's office tomorrow?"

"Yeah," Ernesto confirmed. "Your dad said he's gonna run a different kind of council office than Esposito did. He talked about 'transparency.' He said anybody willing to come down and stand in line can talk to him face to face. So maybe you better warn your dad to get a good night's sleep tonight. Maybe he should meditate or do whatever he does to calm down."

Carmen laughed. "Oh, I'd love to be a fly on the wall when those guys meet. Let me know what happens, Ernie."

"You'll know as soon as your dad gets home," Ernesto chuckled.

When Naomi and Ernesto left school the next day, they went directly to Oriole Street. Ernesto didn't know anybody on the street. So he didn't drive there often. Now, as he turned on Oriole, he was shocked. He was driving twenty-five miles an hour, but he quickly slowed down to ten miles an hour. Even then, the ride was bumpy.

"Look Naomi," Ernesto pointed when he parked. "The blacktop looks like corn-meal or something. After they put in the new water pipes, they just did patchwork."

Naomi took pictures of the worst spots with her phone. "Look at that pothole," she cried. "A small dog could fall in there and not be found for a week." Naomi was exaggerating a little, but the pothole *was* big.

"Picture some kid—a new driver— coming down Oriole in the dark and hitting that pothole," Ernesto commented.

They spotted Eppy's home then. It was a very small green stucco house, well maintained but humble. The yard was filled with geraniums. People can use geranium cuttings to grow new plants. So it was cheap to landscape with geraniums. Eppy and his wife had a loving family, but little in the way of possessions. Many of the other houses on the street were poorly maintained. The yards boasted of nothing green except weeds.

Naomi took a lot of pictures. "This should convince anybody," she declared in a firm voice.

"I wonder what it would cost to repave Oriole and Starling," Ernesto asked out loud. "Probably a million dollars. The city budget is really strapped as it is. But this is a safety issue. This has gotta be taken care of. What if they do nothing, and some kid is killed by an out-of-control car. That would be criminal negligence."

Ernesto drove Naomi down Bluebird Street to pick up her father. Felix Martinez had just gotten home. He turned off the engine of his pickup truck and jumped eagerly from the cab. He had fire in his eyes. "At lunch today," he announced, "I told Eppy what we're doing. He don't think it'll do any good. I don't either. But I told Eppy at least we'll ruin that crook Ibarra's day for him. You got good pictures there, Naomi?"

Naomi showed her father the pictures on her phone. "Great! Beautiful!" Felix Martinez remarked, grinning. "You did a wonderful job. We're gonna shove these pictures in that clown's face. Let's see what he's got to say for himself."

All three of them went into the Martinez house briefly. Felix Martinez changed from his dusty work clothes into a white shirt and slacks. "I don't want that stuffed shirt Ibarra to be looking down on me," he declared. "Guy like him never done an honest day's work in his life. Makes his living dreaming up financial deals. He never went out there in the real world and worked up a sweat, like Eppy and me."

Linda Martinez stood in the living room, looking nervous. "Don't get into any arguments, Felix," she cautioned him. "No name calling. Just state what you came to say and let it go at that."

"Listen to her," Mr. Martinez laughed. "She wants me to kiss Ibarra's foot. 'Hey Mr. Ibarra! You big important jerk! You clown with a mustache! Lissen, you're so much better than me. I should be honored to be in the same room with you. But I beg you, oh great man, would you consider paving Oriole Street?' How's that, Linda? Is that good?"

"Just don't get into any name calling," Mrs. Martinez pleaded. She dreaded getting a call from the police that her husband was in jail for threatening a councilman.

"You mean I can't call him what he is?" Naomi's father asked. "He's a big stupid fool. He's the laughingstock of the whole *barrio*. He puts on a plastic sheriff's badge from the cereal box!"

"Don't worry, Mom," Naomi assured her mother. "It'll be good. All good."

Mrs. Martinez watched her husband, daughter, and Ernesto go out the door. Brutus, the family's pit bull stood beside her. He could tell she was upset. He nuzzled her leg with his head in sympathy. At one time, Linda Martinez feared the dog so much she locked herself in the kitchen when he was loose in the house. Now she loved the dog like a member of the family.

Outside, Ernesto got behind the wheel of the Volvo, and Naomi's father sat beside him. Naomi got in the back.

"I'm thinking, Ernie," Mr. Martinez mused. His voice was throbbing with excitement and anticipation. "This is maybe the beginning of the end for Ibarra. This is when he gets unmasked for the phony hypocrite that he is."

Felix Martinez was really enjoying this adventure. Emilio Ibarra had won the council seat once held by Monte Esposito, Felix's beloved cousin. Mr. Martinez hated

Ibarra from the moment he announced he was running. When Ibarra got elected, Felix Martinez hated him even more. But it was a powerless hatred. Mr. Martinez could do nothing about the election results.

Now Felix Martinez had a chance to bring Ibarra down. Now maybe Emilio Ibarra could be ousted. "Ernie, you gotta ask your Uncle Arturo, the lawyer guy, something. What's the deal with getting a councilman recalled? I think, you know, you gotta get so many signatures or something on a petition. I don't know that much about it. But your uncle would know, bein' a lawyer. You call him, Ernie, and get the scoop on that."

Naomi's dad lapsed into deep thought for a minute. "We could gather the signatures and get a recall election going. You know, like they did with that governor we had. He was kind of a dud, but this Ibarra, he's worse. We oughta be able to get a lotta signatures fast. Then this phony bunch of lies against my cousin can get settled. He can get found innocent of those trumped-up bribery charges. All he gotta do is run again for his old seat. He'll be right back on the city council."

In the back seat, Naomi sighed. Ernesto glanced back at her when he was stopped for a red light. Their gazes met, and both of them smiled.

"Watch him call those deputy sheriffs the minute he sees me," Felix Martinez declared gleefully. "He's afraid of me, you know. He's a big tall dude, but he's a coward. I got more courage in my little finger than he's got in his whole body. I wish the newspeople would be there. Wouldn't it be great if he had us all thrown out of there and it was on the TV tonight?"

"Let's hope it doesn't come to that," Naomi suggested.

"Hey!" Naomi's father exclaimed. "This might be a good thing. Let the fools out there who elected Ibarra see what a liar he is. He invites people down to bring their problems. Then when he don't like who comes, he gets them thrown out."

Ernesto pulled into the parking lot designated for city hall visitors. The lot wasn't too crowded.

"I bet most of the people goin' in to see that fool Ibarra ain't even got cars," Mr. Martinez remarked. "They're bums from the ravine. Or they're sleeping on the street and looking to for government handouts. They don't want to work. So guys like Ibarra raise our taxes so they can give more to the bums. Ibarra wants to look like this big generous guy who helps the poor. But he won't pave that lousy Oriole Street so a hardworking guy like Eppy doesn't bust up his truck."

The trio walked into the government building. They checked the directory on the ground floor. It listed the offices for council members, the mayor, and the city manager. They were all on the third floor.

On the third floor, the three visitors found Councilman Ibarra's office. "Boy," Mr. Martinez growled, "look there at Ibarra's nameplate—'Emilio Zapata Ibarra.'

He's got the whole thing there. He thinks he's the biggest thing on the planet. He's a jerk who ran around the *barrio* scaring kids with his silly plastic badge. I still can't believe those fools voted out a great man like my cousin and put this jerk in his seat."

About eight people stood in line outside Mr. Ibarra's door. That was how the open Thursdays were run. No one made an appointment. People just came between two and four, the earlier the better. They stood in line until one of the councilman's aides invited them in. Ernesto had heard that sometimes the deadline of four o'clock was ignored. Mr. Ibarra continued seeing people until well past eight o'clock. He tried not to turn anyone away.

Four of the waiting group were well-dressed men. One was a nicely dressed lady. Three looked as though they had slept in their clothing.

"Get a load of them," Mr. Martinez murmured under his breath. "There's them from the ravine. Maybe they want Ibarra to buy them sleeping bags so they're more cozy under their tarps. I told you they'd be here."

A young man was taking the names of those who were waiting. As he took names, the aide also asked for the topic to be discussed. The poorly dressed men said they were getting the runaround at the local community clinic.

"They want their free drugs," Mr. Martinez whispered to Ernesto and Naomi. "Yeah, that's what they're looking for. Ibarra is just the one to give them out too. Long as you don't work, you're a *Zapatista*."

Ernesto looked at Naomi. They were both having second thoughts about the wisdom of coming down here with Felix Martinez. Ernesto wished he and Naomi had come alone. Maybe, they were both thinking, Linda Martinez and Luis Sandoval had been right about being worried.

The aide to Councilman Ibarra stopped alongside Mr. Martinez with his yellow legal pad. He asked, "You are—?"

"Felix Martinez," he replied in a loud enough voice for everyone to hear. "I'm a hardworking man who pays his taxes. Lately I've been paying a lot of taxes. Property taxes, sales taxes, income taxes. Yeah, they're wanting guys like me to turn their pockets inside out. That's so the ones who ain't too interested in working can get their 'needs met.'" Mr. Martinez put special emphasis on the last two words. "I didn't come here for no handouts though. I come here for justice."

He turned and said, "This is my daughter, Naomi. This here is her friend, Ernesto Sandoval."

The young man look perplexed as he wrote down the names. "And you're all here on the same problem?" he asked.

"Yeah," Naomi's dad asserted, "we need to get Oriole and Starling streets paved. It's falling apart down there. It's a safety hazard on those streets. That windbag in there—Ibarra—he needs to hear about it. How the mufflers are fallin' out of the cars and laying there like dead animals. Them streets're as rotten as the city dump."

Ernesto grabbed Naomi's hand to comfort her.

CHAPTER SEVEN

The other people in line seemed to take care of their business with Mr. Ibarra quickly. The homeless man who went last took the longest, but he came out smiling.

"He got what he wanted," Mr. Martinez mumbled grimly. "More of my tax money out the window. Maybe Ibarra gave him a coupla twenties so he could load up on vodka."

The door to the councilman's office opened. There sat Emilio Zapata Ibarra behind a nice walnut desk, wearing a T-shirt and jeans. Monte Esposito had always worn a business suit and tie.

"Well, good afternoon Mr. Martinez," Ibarra greeted him. "Naomi, Ernesto. Sit down. Sit down. What can I do for you today?"

"This ain't no social visit," Felix Martinez growled, looking at the other man with contempt. "We got a serious problem out on Oriole and Starling streets, Ibarra. And you better do something about it."

"Mr. Martinez," Emilio Ibarra corrected him. "I know that we have never been friends. But I do expect civil behavior. Please do not address me as Ibarra. It is *Mister* Ibarra, or Councilman Ibarra, or even Emilio. I do believe I am owed some respect. Okay?"

"Oh hey, a thousand pardons," Felix Martinez declared with mock contrition. "Maybe I should call you Potentate Ibarra. Hey, your mustache is looking a little reddish. You didn't get some spaghetti sauce trapped in there, did you?"

Mr. Ibarra's mustache twitched ever so slightly. Ernesto noticed it and hurried to change the conversation. "Councilman, you probably know that new water pipes were installed on Oriole Street and on Starling Street—" he began.

"He don't know nothin' about water pipes in the *barrio*!" Naomi's father cut Ernesto off. "He's got this cushy job here now. All he needs to do is sit behind his desk and look important. Hey, speakin' of that, how come you're not wearing your plastic sheriff's badge today? You know, the one you got from the cereal box. I always seen you running around the neighborhood scaring the kiddies with that badge."

The councilman glared at Mr. Martinez for a moment and then looked back at Ernesto. "And," Ernesto continued desperately, his voice strained, "after they put in the water pipes, they repaved the streets. But they didn't do such a hot job. The surfaces of Oriole and Starling streets are rutted and dangerous now."

"Like this stuffed shirt cares," Mr. Martinez sneered. "He don't care what's goin' on down on Oriole Street. He lives on

Nuthatch Lane, and everything's cool down there. Come to think of it, that's a good street for this guy to live on. Nuts get hatched there."

Mr. Ibarra's face reddened, and his mustache danced a little more. Naomi spoke up. "I've taken pictures of the street on my phone," She held the phone out to Mr. Ibarra, flipping through the photos. "You can see the terrible condition of the paving. I took a picture of this one pothole . . . right . . . here." Naomi clicked through several pictures on her phone. "This one is on Oriole. I think thousands of dollars of damage are done to cars that have to use that street—or Starling. And, if a car were to hit one of the ruts and lose control, somebody could get hurt or killed."

Mr. Ibarra took Naomi's phone and flipped intently through the pictures.

" 'Course," Mr. Martinez remarked, "those guys from the ravine don't live on Oriole. Or else maybe there'd be some action. Just poor hardworking stiffs like

Eppy Pastro, guys with lower-middle-class salaries. Those guys work like dogs all their lives, and they have to live on a street that's a death trap."

By now, the councilman had tuned out Felix Martinez's insults. Now Naomi's dad was only background noise, like a vacuum cleaner or construction sounds.

"When were the new water pipes installed?" Mr. Ibarra asked Naomi.

"See," Naomi's father crowed, "the guy don't know nothin'. He's just sittin' there keeping his chair warm."

"Six months ago," Ernesto answered. "It wasn't too bad at first. Then it rained, and the street just crumbled."

"Let them whistle for all this jerk cares," Mr. Martinez snarled.

Emilio Ibarra's mustache visibly jumped. The councilman had had enough. He rose to his feet. He was about the same height as Mr. Martinez. But he was a more formidable-looking man, with his heavy black mustache, bushy black eyebrows, and thick, long hair. "I don't have to sit here and take your abuse, Martinez. If you can't behave like a civilized person, you can just get out of my office," Mr. Ibarra commanded, shouting.

"See," Felix Martinez gloated, looking at the teenagers. "What did I tell you? Here it comes. What did I say? He don't want to do nothin' about Oriole Street. He just wants to be the big shot councilman enjoying the perks. Didn't I tell you guys he wouldn't want to listen to us?"

Mr. Martinez turned to Councilman Ibarra, "These kids worked for you during the campaign, joined that *Zapatista* group. They thought you were this great big hope for the *barrio*. They worked against a great councilman, Monte Esposito. They wouldn't listen to reason."

Turning back to Naomi and Ernesto, Felix Martinez spoke to them. "See what we got here now, you guys? This big fat nothing of a guy with a crazy mustache sittin' on his fat—"

"Get out of my office, Felix Martinez," Mr. Ibarra ordered. "I'm not joking. I don't have to be insulted like this by some Neanderthal!"

"Ha!" Naomi's father cried. "It's getting' better! Now he calls me a caveman just because I'm fighting for the poor guys over on Oriole. And all they want is a street they can drive on. Beautiful!"

"Come on, Dad," Naomi urged, gently grasping her father's arm. "Let's go. We said our piece and—"

Mr. Martinez jerked free of his daughter's grasp. "Why don't you get the deputy sheriffs to drag us away, Ibarra? You better do that. We're bad people. We're just hardworking stiffs who want what's right. That's dangerous. Oooooo! We're baaad!"

He leaned over to Ernesto and whispered to him. "Ernie, go see if there's any newspeople around. See if you can get them in here for the show. Tell them some good pictures are coming up for the evening TV. Democracy in action."

Naomi seemed to be in a daze. But her words came out with surprising clarity. "Mr. Ibarra, do you want me to e-mail these pictures to your office?" she asked. "You can look at them further . . . uh . . . when you get a chance."

Emilio Ibarra looked at her and answered in a fairly calm voice. "Yes, thank you. I would appreciate that."

" 'Cause there's no one on Oriole Street with enough money to bribe you guys to do the right thing," Felix Martinez taunted. "That's the problem."

Ernesto tried to keep Mr. Ibarra's attention. "I understand," he said, "that the city council will be voting on the city's paving issue next Tuesday in the late afternoon."

"That is . . . correct," Councilman Ibarra responded. He looked as though he was about to say more, but Naomi spoke up.

"Let's go, Dad," Naomi said. "We've made our case as much as we can."

"Ha!" her father exclaimed. "Like anything we said makes any difference to

130

this joker here. He's laughing up his sleeve right now."

Felix Martinez was now shouting so loud that he was frightening the people waiting in the hall. To some of them, the world was dangerous and unpredictable. They feared something terrible might be going on in the councilman's office.

The office door opened, and everyone's head turned toward it. Two large deputy sheriffs stood in the doorway.

Felix Martinez looked delighted. He looked like a child at Christmastime watching Santa Claus as he placed gifts under the tree.

"See?" Mr. Martinez shouted. "Here we go! Democracy in action. The people want to speak, and the heavy hand of the law is brought in to silence them. Is this the United States of America? What's happened to my country? I want my country back!"

One of the deputies looked at Councilman Ibarra and asked, "Do you need us, sir?"

Mr. Ibarra sat down heavily. "No, no," he sighed, his hand raised to wave the men off. "Everything is fine. We were just having a spirited discussion on the subject of potholes. Thank you, gentlemen, for checking on us. But it's all just fine. Excellent. Mr. Martinez here is a very colorful personality. He tends to talk in a very loud voice. But he's leaving now. Good afternoon, Mr. Martinez, Naomi, Ernesto. It was indeed a pleasure. Such a pleasure . . ." The councilman sat shaking his head slowly.

As the three of them left the office, Felix Martinez looked disappointed. He wanted to escalate the confrontation. He figured it would have been worth it to be handcuffed and thrown into jail. No charges would have been filed, of course. But maybe he could have appeared on the nightly news. He felt as though he'd missed a chance to vent his rage and frustration against Councilman Ibarra.

"Well," Mr. Martinez gloated cheerfully as they walked to the Volvo, "we ruined his day."

"To say nothing of our day," Ernesto mumbled in a soft voice that only Naomi could hear.

When Mr. Martinez was in the car, he declared, "Of course, nothing'll come of it. Those crooks, led by Ibarra, will vote on Tuesday. The paving project'll be shelved for further study. That's what they always do. They ain't got the guts to just kill it. Just bury it in a bottom drawer and hope the fools out there forget about it."

The man chuckled. "You know, though, it was great goin' eyeball to eyeball with that fraud. That was my first chance since he stole Monte's seat on the city council." Dad pulled out his cell phone and called Eppy.

"Hey Eppy!" Mr. Martinez crowed into the phone. "We did it. We went down to that crook's office and scared the daylights out of him. He was shakin' in his boots, man. He couldn't believe someone had enough courage to confront him in his own little lair. It was like in the movies, you know, high noon at the OK Corral. He was sweatin' Eppy. He calls for these deputy sheriffs then. He wanted us arrested. But those guys saw what was goin' on. They wouldn't slap the cuffs on decent citizens for nothin'. The sheriffs just stood there. Decent guys. They were okay."

Ernesto was stopped for a light when he glanced back at Naomi. She was resting her chin in her hands, laughing silently.

"What's that, Eppy?" Mr. Martinez asked. "Do I think Ibarra will vote to repave Oriole? Not a chance. He's a crook and a phony. Naomi got these great pictures of your street. Showed them to the bum. Nothin'. But listen, Eppy. Ernie here, he's got this uncle who's a lawyer. He's gonna look into getting a recall going on Ibarra. Yeah. Maybe we can get the bum out of office. Ernie's gonna work on that with his uncle. We'll get our petitions and have a recall."

Eppy said something like, "That's great, Felix."

Mr. Martinez just went on talking. "Yep! And the best thing is, my cousin just has to get out from under all those false charges they got against him. Then he's back in office before we know it."

It sounded as though Eppy was thanking his friend. "Yeah," Naomi's dad replied. "You bet, Eppy. We fought the good fight, and we ain't giving up."

When Mr. Martinez closed the phone, he suggested, "How about us getting some frozen yogurt at Chill Out? After the day we had, I could use that." Mr. Martinez seemed in a happy, outgoing mood.

"Sure, Dad," Naomi agreed. Ernesto turned the Volvo in the direction of the frozen yogurt shop.

It seemed strange to Naomi to be going into Chill Out when she wasn't working. But the trio sat down, and Sherry served them frozen chocolate yogurts.

Felix Martinez looked at Ernesto. "Hey, Ernie, I really appreciate how you come along with us today and stood by us. Makes me feel good that you done that."

"Yes, well," Ernesto hesitated. "I'm glad . . . I could . . . be there, you know. I hope Oriole gets paved."

"Nah, won't happen. But we tried," Mr. Martinez asserted.

As they sat eating their yogurt, Naomi's dad called Orlando. He told his son the whole story, embellishing even more than he did with Eppy. In this latest version, Mr. Ibarra was crouched in terror behind his desk. When he got off the phone, Felix Martinez grinned and said, "Orlando got a big kick out of that. He was laughing. You shoulda heard him laughing. Man, it's good to have my boys back in the fold."

He turned to Naomi. "It's all your doing, baby. You're my angel."

As they walked out of Chill Out, Mr. Martinez pointed. "Hey, look at that fancy car over there. BMW, right?"

Naomi stared at the car and turned numb. It was Elia Ancho's BMW. He was supposed to be in Mexico with his daughters. He was supposed to be getting help for his aggression and depression problems. What was he doing back here?

Elia Ancho stepped from the car and walked toward the trio. "You know that guy?" Naomi's father asked her.

"Yes, that's Mr. Ancho. He owns Chill Out," Naomi answered in a faltering voice.

"Hello there, Naomi," Mr. Ancho called to her when he was close. He stared at Naomi's father and Ernesto. Naomi felt she had to introduce them.

"Mr. Ancho," she began, "this is my dad, Felix Martinez. And you've seen Ernesto Sandoval, the boy who picks me up. Mr. Ancho owns the yogurt shop, and his son Jimmy is the manager, Dad."

"Well, glad to meet you, Mr. Martinez," Mr. Ancho said, extending his hand. "You have a wonderful daughter here. She is the best employee we have. Congratulations on raising such a fine young woman."

Felix Martinez smiled broadly and took the man's hand. "Oh hey, thanks a lot, Mr. Ancho. Naomi loves working here. Yeah, she's always saying how nice everybody is. I can see what she means just by meeting you."

When Mr. Ancho continued on into Chill Out, Naomi's father commented, "Now there's a fine gentleman. You can see that right away. And he thinks highly of you, Naomi. A compliment like that coming from a real high-class guy like that, it means a lot."

"Yes," Naomi replied, climbing into the backseat of the car. She closed her eyes. It had been a nerve-wracking afternoon. Now this. Naomi was scheduled to work tomorrow. She didn't know whether she could cope with Mr. Ancho being there at his regular table. He seemed so nice and normal right now. Yet she couldn't forget that incident when he almost choked a boy to death.

Naomi was glad when her father went in the house on Bluebird Street. She had some time alone with Ernesto to talk about what had just happened at Chill Out.

"Babe," Ernesto suggested, "maybe the guy went to the doctor. Maybe they gave him antidepressants, and he's settled down. That happens sometimes. But I could get someone to fill in for me at the pizzeria tomorrow. Then I could sort of hang around when I take you to work. I'll have some frozen yogurts, go out, amble back in. I'll keep my eye on you all evening."

"Oh Ernie," Naomi protested. "I don't want you missing work. Maybe Mr. Ancho won't even come in tomorrow. And you're right about medications working miracles. There was a guy on our street a few years back. He was really manic. He went on medications and went back to work. He was fine."

"Well," Ernesto acceded, "we'll play it by ear, babe. I just don't want you to worry about it. If he comes in, sits for a few minutes and then leaves, that's fine. But if he starts watching you . . ."

"Okay Ernie," Naomi assured him, leaning over and kissing him goodnight. "Love you forever."

"Me too," Ernesto responded. "Hey! Ms. D'Cruz announces who's playing Cesar Chavez and Dolores Huerta tomorrow after class."

"Oh, in all the excitement, I almost forgot about that," Naomi said.

"I have a good feeling that we'll be working together on that, babe," Ernesto told her.

"Well, if I do get it, Orlando and Manny promised to come down and help me," she said. "I told them I'd make sure Mom made *carne asada*."

CHAPTER EIGHT

Naomi went into the house. Dad was telling Mom how he brought Emilio Ibarra to his knees. Linda Martinez had a look of pure misery on her face. She was in the Legion of Mary at Our Lady of Guadalupe Church with Conchita Ibarra. Now she'd be embarrassed to go to the meeting on Saturday. Linda Martinez could just imagine what Emilio was telling Conchita tonight about his meeting. But in spite of how she felt inside, Mrs. Martinez listened to Felix's rant. She smiled and nodded at the appropriate times, as if what he had done was wonderful.

As her mom listened politely to her dad, Naomi went into the kitchen to clean up. Mom had made fish tacos for Felix and Zack.

A little later, Mrs. Martinez joined her daughter in the kitchen. "Oh Naomi," Mom said in a soft voice barely above a whisper. "It must have been terrible for you and Ernie down there at Mr. Ibarra's office."

"Oh well," Naomi shrugged, "me and Ernie got the message across. I downloaded the pictures I took to Mr. Ibarra's computer. He liked that."

"Your father," Linda Martinez asked, fearful of the answer. "Was he . . . terrible?"

Naomi didn't know what to say. "Uh, he was, well, you know, Mom . . . forceful."

"What you're saying is that he was terrible," Mom said, shaking her head. "I'll be so ashamed to face Conchita at the meeting on Saturday."

"Don't worry about it, Mom," Naomi consoled her. "I gotta face Carmen at school. But they understand. I mean, it is what it is."

"Now he's talking about getting a petition going," Mom stated. "He wants to recall Mr. Ibarra and put his crooked cousin back in office. Good heavens, Monte Esposito was indicted for bribery by a grand jury!"

"Yeah," Naomi told her mother, "he was after poor Ernie to get his Uncle Arturo to get the ball rolling. Of course that's not going anywhere."

Mom looked at Naomi with fright in her eyes. "But what if on Tuesday the city council turns down paving those streets? What if Mr. Ibarra votes that way too? The other morning I brought Meals on Wheels to a ninety-year-old lady on Oriole Street. I hit something uneven in the street. I thought I'd broken the springs on the Toyota. It *is* a dreadful situation"

The next morning, Naomi sent the photos to the e-mail address on the town Web site. Then she biked to school. She hoped she wouldn't run into Carmen Ibarra. But just as Naomi was locking up her bike, Carmen came running toward her. "Oh no!" Naomi thought. "Carmen's going to say how angry her father is about Dad's rudeness. What am I supposed to say? I know Daddy acted awful, but he's my father and I love him. He embarrasses the life out of me several times a week. But I'm stuck with him."

"Hi Naomi," Carmen hailed. "Today we find out if you're Dolores. I hope you are!"

Naomi blinked. "Uh well, yeah, today's the day. Uh . . . Carmen, about yesterday . . . I'm really sorry." Naomi thought she had to say something. Carmen was a dear friend. They'd been friends since first grade. She had to tell Carmen how sorry she was about how Dad acted toward her father.

"Oh yeah," Carmen responded, "that sandwich you gave me. It was kinda dry, but it was okay. It was my fault for forgetting my own lunch again. I appreciate that you shared with me." Carmen giggled then. "I didn't think you still ate peanut butter and jelly sandwiches!"

Then Carmen noticed the strange expression on Naomi's face. "What's the matter?"

"Oh Carmen," Naomi blurted. "Dad was so rude and nasty in your dad's office yesterday. I'm really sorry, Carmen. I'm so embarrassed."

"Oh, don't worry about that," Carmen told her, laughing. "My dad embarrasses me all the time too. How do you think I feel when he wears that plastic sheriff's badge while people are around. He used to march down the street with that on. He terrorized the middle schoolers when I was in middle school."

Carmen giggled again. "Oh Naomi, I was so humiliated. I begged Mom to homeschool me so I wouldn't have to face the kids anymore. Mom said she couldn't because then I'd grow up a dummy. I told her it was better to be a dummy. All my friends asked me, "That crazy guy with the big mustache and the plastic badge from the cereal box. Is he your dad?"

"But your father is better now," Naomi objected.

145

"So is yours, most of the time," Carmen said.

"Did your dad say anything last night about what happened in his office?" Naomi asked.

"Yeah," Carmen nodded. "He said you had really good pictures of Oriole Street, and Ernie was very polite. Then Dad said Felix Martinez is kind of a madman. But then he admitted he was sort of a madman too. He said maybe it's something in the water we get in the *barrio*."

Naomi felt much better. Carmen could always make her feel better. When the girls were ten years old, they had made a pact. When one of them got married, the other would be a bridesmaid at the wedding. Naomi didn't have a better friend in the whole school than Carmen Ibarra.

Naomi's last class of the day was speech. She was scheduled to make a speech describing how to make something. One boy described how to make a good turkey sandwich. That went over big. Now it was Naomi's turn. She couldn't think of anything to make. So she made an origami stork. Clay Aguirre was in the class, and he laughed at her. "That is so lame," he crowed. "Is this third grade or what?"

The speech teacher, Ms. Hawley, was kind of deaf. She didn't hear Clay's insult, but she saw him laughing. The teacher glared at him as Naomi hurried back to her seat, clutching her origami stork.

She was thinking about Ms. D'Cruz's upcoming announcements about the Cesar Chavez birthday program. They would be made over the school's PA system at the very end of the last class of the day. She was in no mood to hear that she wasn't going to be Dolores Huerta. Her father would only have yet another reason to be mad.

When Ms. D'Cruz's bubbly voice came over the PA system, Naomi felt like crawling under her desk.

"We want to thank all the talented students," the teacher began, "who tried out for the Cesar Chavez birthday program. All of you will be doing singing or speaking roles. To play the part of Cesar Chavez, we have chosen junior Ernesto Sandoval. Speaking and singing the part of Dolores Huerta will be junior Naomi Martinez."

The PA clicked off. Students all over the school filed out of the classrooms.

Naomi remained in her seat. She couldn't believe what she'd just heard. Only when her friends surrounded her, congratulating her, did she believe it. And then Ernesto looked in the classroom door, grinning, and called out, "Hi Dolores!"

When Naomi got home from school, her father was on the phone with Monte Esposito. "Next Tuesday, it's all comin' down Monte," he promised. "Ernie, Naomi's guy, he and his buddies are comin' down to the city council with me and Eppy. We'll just wait till Ibarra votes with the other crooks against repaving Oriole. Then the kids are gonna yell and stamp their feet in protest. We'll probably all get thrown out. Might be on TV. It'll cook Ibarra's goose. Then we can get the recall stuff goin'."

Naomi stood there in silence until her father was off the phone. Then she said, "Hi, Dad."

"Hi beautiful," Felix Martinez said. "I hope you had a good day." Naomi's father had always been fairly nice to her, But since she got the family reconciled, he was sweeter than ever. Nothing Naomi could have done would have meant as much as healing the family rift.

"Daddy, I'm Dolores," Naomi announced.

For a minute, her father didn't seem to know what she was talking about. He wanted her to win the role of Dolores Huerta. He even asked Ernesto to make sure she tried out. But he'd been so wrapped up trying to unseat Emilio Ibarra that he could scarcely think of anything else. Then it dawned on him. "You got the part?" he yelled.

"Yes, Daddy," Naomi gushed with a giggle.

Felix Martinez sprinted across the room to where Naomi was standing. He grabbed her, lifted her off her feet, and swung her around. Her father kissed her and said, "Oh baby, that's beautiful. You'll be great! You'll be in the spotlight where you belong." Then he started shouting, "Linda! Linda! Get out here. Naomi got the part of Dolores in the school . . . thing. They chose our little girl. Naomi's gonna be the girl everybody is looking at. I'm so proud of you, baby—so proud!"

Mom came from the kitchen. She'd been making a pie, and her hands were covered with flour. But she grabbed Naomi too and hugged and kissed her. Naomi didn't care about the smudges of flour all over her top.

When the excitement died down, Naomi called Orlando. He promised to come down to help her prepare for her singing role.

Then Naomi got ready for work. She tried to keep Mr. Ancho out of her mind. She told herself that seeing him going into Chill Out didn't mean anything. It didn't mean he'd be sitting at the table watching her. He probably was just in and out of the store.

Ernesto did get someone to take his shift at the pizzeria. He took Naomi to work and hung around all evening. He told Naomi he'd be working on his laptop computer in the Volvo, doing a book report. Mr. Ancho never showed up. Jimmy mentioned that he was back from Mexico, but he was now on medication. He promised not to visit Chill Out for a while. Naomi began to worry less.

Ernesto Sandoval had promised that he and his friends would show up Tuesday at city hall. That was when the city council was going to vote on repaving Oriole and Starling streets. He kept his promise. Felix Martinez led the way, driving Eppy in the pickup. Following was Ernesto, driving the Volvo with Paul Morales, Carmen's boyfriend, and two other boys from Chavez High. The two boys, Dom Reynosa and Carlos Negrete, had been tagger dropouts. Then Ernesto's father rescued them from the street and brought them back into the junior class.

"You guys," Ernesto announced, "we want the city council, and especially Councilman Ibarra, to vote for repaving those rundown streets. If they don't, we're gonna make a loud noise. Got it?"

"Most of the houses on Oriole are dumps," Paul Morales pointed out. "The venerable city fathers don't care much about folks living in dumps. I think we're gonna get the chance to make a scene."

"Yeah," Dom added. "Politicians like people who got money to donate to their campaigns. I don't think anybody on Oriole or Starling gave lately to Ibarra's coffers or anybody else's."

Carlos agreed. "My father hates politicians. When one comes on the TV, he grabs the remote and zaps him. Mosta them are crooks. They don't care about nobody but themselves."

"Yeah," Ernesto agreed. "But Emilio Ibarra is supposed to be different. Already he's done some good things. I'm not giving up on the guy yet. He's gotta prove to me that he's no good. I supported him. I was a *Zapatista*, and I hate to think I was taken in." Ernesto glanced over at Paul, who sat beside him. "I'm even thinking about getting to be a lawyer. Maybe I'll run for office myself someday."

"You want your turn at the trough, huh Ernie?" Dom laughed.

"No," Ernesto protested. "It doesn't have to be that way. We can't just accept that this is the way it is, that we can't do any better. You gotta believe that good men and women out there really want to help the people and help the country. I mean, our family's patriotic. Dad served in Iraq. He risked his life 'cause he loves this country. A lot of people do. That's why maybe someday I'll be a politician—a good one."

"I don't know," Carlos said. "People used to think old Monte Esposito was a good guy. Now he's trying to cut a deal with the district attorney on those bribery charges. All the swell furniture in his house? The news is sayin' it all came from dudes he'd done favors for when he was on the council. Yeah, lot of us thought Ibarra would be different. But who knows? I guess today we're gonna find out. If he won't even vote to save little old Oriole Street, then he's not the guy we hoped he was."

Ernesto parked right next to Felix Martinez's pickup truck. Naomi's father and his friend Eppy got out of the truck. Mr. Martinez looked fired up, like he was expecting a battle. The six of them walked to the city building and rode the elevator up to council chambers.

Ernesto had been to city council meetings before with his civics class. The teacher had taken the kids downtown to see city government in action. They watched the mayor presiding over a discussion on whether to brown out the fire department to save money. Ernesto knew "browning out" meant closing down some of the fire stations for a while. The purchase of certain fire engines would be put on hold. Ernesto remembered he didn't pay much attention to the proceedings. He was thinking about Naomi the whole time.

But today Ernesto would be paying attention.

Felix Martinez, Eppy, and the four boys found good seats near the front of the room with a good view of the city council. Of the eight members, three were women and five were men, including Mr. Ibarra. Ernesto didn't know much about any of them. He just had never been interested. Now he stared intently at Emilio Ibarra. Ernesto hoped that, when all was said and done, he wouldn't turn out to be another Monte Esposito.

Felix Martinez looked over at Ernesto and the other boys. "You guys, this is gonna be a bitter lesson," he advised. "It's good for you, though. We went down to Ibarra's office and gave him proof that those streets are dangerous to ride on. Naomi even took pictures. He's got the evidence. Now you're gonna see democracy in action." Mr. Martinez's voice dripped with sarcasm. "Now you're gonna see what's wrong in the United States of America."

CHAPTER NINE

All the members of the city council were finally seated, along with the mayor and city manager. The mayor was the chairperson for the meeting. The city manager acted as the secretary. Some routine procedural business was done.

The group sat through discussion and votes on routine business. A traffic light was approved for a busy intersection downtown. New housing was put up at the edge of town, and the trash pickup schedule had to be changed. The local Little League subsidy was approved. A boring hour or more passed. The group began to think they'd never get their chance to speak.

Then, finally, the mayor spoke to everyone in the chamber. "Ladies and gentlemen," he began. He leaned in slightly to the microphone on the table in front of him. "Welcome to all of you who came tonight. Those with approval to speak on various issues will be heard as soon as one very pressing matter is handled. Councilman Ibarra has asked that it be addressed promptly. He will be making some opening comments. I yield the floor to Mr. Ibarra."

Councilman Emilio Ibarra scooted his chair closer to the table with the microphone.

Felix Martinez leaned over to Ernesto. "Silence in the court," he whispered. "The monkey wants to speak."

"Shhh!" Ernesto pleaded.

"Last Thursday," Emilio Ibarra said, "I held my usual open-door session in the afternoon. I was visited by three citizens with an urgent matter. What they had come to discuss was the condition of two streets, Oriole and Starling. The city, it seems, installed new water pipes and repaved the streets with less than perfect results. The adult citizen who brought this to my attention was very . . . uh . . . forceful." Mr. Ibarra's mustache twitched ever so slightly. "But the two teenagers with him were highly informative and convincing."

Felix Martinez looked over at Ernesto. "He's gonna ridicule me in public. You hear that? He's gonna complain how rude I was to his highness. I can't believe this jerk." Naomi's father tightened his hands into fists and pounded them on the arms of his chair.

"The daughter of the gentleman who led the delegation," Mr. Ibarra continued. "supplied pictures of the deteriorated condition of the street. And the young man with them expressed how dangerous travel was on those streets."

The councilman went on. "Later in the afternoon, I drove over to Oriole and Starling streets. I myself saw how dangerous their condition was. The roadbed on either street is an accident waiting to happen. We must treat this as an emergency situation."

Mr. Ibarra had been speaking to the people in the room. Now he looked directly at the mayor and the city board. "As part of this undertaking, I am formally requesting an investigation. We need to know whether the work on those streets was performed according to code. If not, I will seek a refund from the contractor and possibly fines and imprisonment, if need be."

Mr. Ibarra paused a moment, then went on. "You all have the information I provided for you on the cost of the repaving. I am sure you have studied the issue and are now ready to vote. I feel we need a unanimous vote to begin repaving immediately on Oriole and Starling streets."

The mayor thanked the councilman. He then began the formal procedure of taking a vote. "Well, we've heard Councilman Ibarra's comments. Does anyone else have anything to add?" A few members of the council added their comments, all of them in support of repaving and an investigation. When the mayor felt the discussion was complete, he called for the secretary to take a vote.

The city council was unanimous in voting for the repaving project at a cost of nearly a million dollars.

Before anyone in the room could react to the good news, Councilman Ibarra had one more thing to say.

"I see the gentleman who brought this to my attention last Thursday. He's sitting out there in the fourth row. I want to thank you, Señor Felix Martinez. This was a serious and vital issue. I hope you are pleased with the action we took today."

Applause broke out among the spectators, led by Ernesto Sandoval and his three friends. They cheered and stamped their feet.

Felix Martinez sat there like a man brought back from the dead. He stared straight ahead in total shock. He had expected only an announcement that the question had been shelved for further study.

If it was actually brought to a vote, Mr. Martinez expected a ringing defeat. He never thought that Emilio Ibarra would vote for the resolution. And he hardly expected the councilman to lead the charge for it. Finally, Felix Martinez had expected Ibarra to ridicule him before the whole city council. Instead, he heard himself praised and thanked.

The city council began hearing from the people who had come to speak. But Ernesto and his friends left, leading the way out. Felix Martinez and Eppy followed. Mr. Martinez was going very fast, propelling Eppy before him. He was afraid he might somehow run into Emilio Ibarra and be forced to say something civil to him.

But Felix Martinez did not move quickly enough. Emilio Ibarra was in the hall, waiting for him. "Hello there, Felix," he called cheerfully, a big grin making his mustache dance on his upper lip. "We took care of business, didn't we? I was really steamed last Thursday when you came in yelling at me and insulting me. But you know what? You did the right thing coming in. Once I saw those streets, I thought, 'Hey, the guy has a right to be ticked off.' "

Mr. Ibarra held out his hand to Felix Martinez. "You stepped up to the plate. You told me what was going on. Now we can fix things before somebody is really hurt or worse. If more people did that, Felix, government would work a lot better."

"Yeah well," Mr. Martinez muttered, looking at the proffered hand as if it were a poisonous snake. But he took Mr. Ibarra's hand, and they shook. "My friend Eppy here, he was scared. You know, some joker would come flying down Oriole and lose control, maybe kill some of the kids . . . So they're really gonna repave, huh?"

"Yeah, the street department is doing a rush order," Emilio Ibarra assured him. "The trucks will be there before you know it."

Eppy then grasped the councilman's hand too. He did it with fervor. "*Dios le bendiga!*" Eppy told him. "God bless you. *Gracias!*"

"*Por nada*," the councilman replied. His smile grew even wider, and the mustache on his lip did a hula dance.

As Felix Martinez hurried away, Emilio Ibarra called after him. "Anytime you got something to say, Felix, let me know. That's what I'm here for. I love the *barrio*. I was born there, and I'm gonna live there until I die. My heart and soul are in the *barrio* and with the people there. You are my people, and I'm your councilman."

Mr. Martinez walked faster. Ernesto had never seen him looking quite so mortified. He jumped into the pickup with Eppy and took off fast.

"Man!" Paul Morales exclaimed when they were all in the Volvo. "What a turnaround! That politico is awesome. He really listens to people. Naomi's father was getting ready to ream him out, and we were all ready to be boobirds. Then he turns us all around." Paul grinned and shook his head. "I'm sure glad we didn't have to put on a show. I'm on kinda thin ice with Carmen's dad as it is."

"My old man voted for Ibarra," Dom remarked. "This mornin' I was telling him what we thought was gonna happen here today. Dad said if Ibarra turns out rotten, then he's gonna tear up his voter registration. He was never gonna go to the polls again."

Carlos Negrete shook his head in wonderment. "Mr. Martinez told us this was gonna be a bitter lesson in democracy. Yeah, it was a lesson. A good one. You know what, Ernie? There *are* good guys out there. You could be one of them."

"Yeah," Ernesto said, smiling.

After dropping Eppy off at his house, Felix Martinez headed home. It was almost eight o'clock. The Martinez house already smelled of dinner—this time, *carne asada*. The minute the pickup pulled into the driveway, Naomi flew out of the house. "Ernie called me!" she cried. "We won!" She jumped up and down in the driveway, her hands waving over her head. "They're going to repave Oriole and Starling! Daddy, we did it! We went down there and talked to Councilman Ibarra. And it worked! I bet you were thrilled, huh?"

Naomi knew in her heart that her father wasn't thrilled. Dad had already made plans for the recall of the Ibarra election. He wanted to see his crooked cousin's political star rise out of the muck of his misdeeds.

"Yeah, it was a surprise all right," Dad answered slowly. "I guess we really scared the guy into doing the right thing."

"Ernie even said Mr. Ibarra thanked you for bringing the problem to his attention, Dad," Naomi added.

"Yeah, well . . ." Naomi's father mumbled forlornly.

When Naomi and her father got into the house, Linda Martinez tried to cheer up her husband. "Naomi told me what happened down at the city council. Oh, Felix, I'm so proud of you. You went down there and demanded they take care of a bad problem. More people should be like that, Felix."

Then Mom told him, "I've made you one of your favorite dinners. It's almost ready."

"Yeah, good," Felix Martinez replied. Naomi and Mom both knew that it would take more than *carne asada* to cheer him up.

Naomi had seen no sign of Mr. Ancho when she worked on Friday or Monday. Now, arriving with Ernesto on Wednesday, she was happy to see no BMW in the parking lot. Naomi was beginning to rest easy. "I think he's really gone," Naomi told Ernesto. "Jimmy made it clear to his father that he should stay away from Chill Out."

"Well, before quitting time tonight, I'll be back here, babe," Ernesto assured her. "Let me know if you see the guy come in and he's acting strange, you know, spying on you. Call me on my cell, and I'll be here. I don't want you taking any chances."

"Okay, babe," Naomi agreed, leaning over for her kiss. She didn't feel worried.

CHAPTER NINE

When Naomi walked into Chill Out, she saw Sherry Carranza and Jimmy engaged in a friendly conversation at the counter. A family with two little kids sat in a booth. Otherwise the place was empty. The crowd would come in later. It had been a warm day with Santa Ana winds blowing. It was still warm, a perfect evening for frozen yogurt.

"Hey Naomi," Sherry greeted her. "Ready to dish out yogurt?"

"Always!" Naomi answered, putting on her snowman T-shirt and getting behind the counter.

Just then Paul Morales and Carmen Ibarra came in. "Paul was telling me what happened down at city hall on Tuesday," Carmen said. She giggled before ordering two pistachio yogurts. "That musta been a scream. Your poor dad, Naomi. He's all ready to run my dad out of office. Now they're good buddies!"

"Oh it's hard all right," Naomi agreed, laughing too. "He was on the phone to cousin Monte. He was telling Monte that they needed to put the 'recall Ibarra' campaign on hold for a while. My father doesn't like to admit it when he's wrong. You just don't tell him, 'I told you so.'"

"You should've seen the look on your dad's face when the repaving resolution passed with Ibarra's blessing," Paul Morales said to Naomi.

"I was tempted to give Dad one of my old *Zapatista* buttons from the campaign," Naomi said, devilishly. "I was gonna ask him if he'd like to wear it now that Emilio Ibarra is doing the right thing. But Dad has absolutely no sense of humor when it comes to stuff like that."

Later, after Paul and Carmen had left, there were only a few customers. Jimmy Ancho came over and spoke softly to Naomi. "I know my dad stopped by here the other night. He said he had some words with your dad, Naomi. I was really shocked that he flew back from Mexico. But we had a long talk, my father and I, and I told him firmly that he was to stay away from here.

I told him it was best if he stayed completely away. He accepted that. I told him to get together with his old friends and pick up on golf. He used to love to play golf. I don't think there will be any more problems."

"That's good," Naomi replied. "He really is a nice man. He was very cordial to Dad. Dad was very impressed by him."

"I'm glad to hear that, Naomi," Jimmy responded. "But he must stay away. I told him I was handling the business just fine. He needs to take care of himself now. So, Naomi, thanks for being so understanding. And, well, keep up the good work. I hear nothing but good about you from the customers. Our little customer opinion box is jam-packed with good comments about you." Jimmy smiled and went into the back room.

Naomi felt good about the conversation. Mr. Ancho seemed to be out of the picture. She didn't have to worry about him anymore. And all that good feedback about

Naomi's performance at Chill Out was a major ego boost.

As she wiped down a counter, Naomi started thinking about her brothers coming on the weekend. They were going to help her with her music for the school celebration. She was getting excited about playing Dolores Huerta. She used to enjoy singing in her brothers' garage band. Some of that joy was seeping back into her heart. Ernesto was right, she thought. He was mostly always right. It would be fun working with him on the Cesar Chavez birthday celebration.

With about an hour left in her shift, Naomi saw Clay Aguirre come in with Mira Nuñez. Mira was wearing really nice jeans and a striped pullover. She looked striking. She was a very pretty girl and smart too. She earned almost all As. She was also the junior class vice president, and she was popular with the other students.

These days, Clay ignored Naomi most of the time. Ernesto Sandoval had had a serious talk with Clay, telling him to leave

Naomi alone. Yes, once in a while Clay gave her a dirty look. And once he made fun of her in speech class when she did her origami demonstration. But generally he seemed to be into Mira, and Naomi was glad of that. He never parked across the street from her house on Bluebird Street anymore. He no longer shined his flashlight at her window. When he came into Chill Out, he tried to get somebody other than Naomi to wait on him. Tonight, for example, Naomi saw him cross over to place his order with Sherry, even though Naomi's line was open.

Naomi was glad that Clay had finally accepted that they were done.

"What'll we have, babe?" Clay asked Mira as they stood in Sherry's line.

Mira looked at Clay almost worshipfully. She was really stuck on him. "Whatever you want, Clay," she said. "You always pick just the right flavors."

Clay put his arm around Mira and ordered blueberry yogurt with blueberries on the top. He leaned over and kissed her neck. She giggled. When Sherry gave them their yogurts, they walked to a nearby booth.

Naomi was able to overhear most of their conversation, even though she wasn't trying to. Clay spoke in a loud voice. "Man, it's good to be playing football again," he announced.

"I'm so glad," Mira responded. "You're so good at playing. And you look so cool in that football uniform."

Naomi thought Mira sounded like some stupid girl enamored with a creepy jock. Mira was pretty, bright, and a school officer. Yet around Clay she seemed to turn into a simpering fool. But Naomi wasn't too fast to judge Mira. After all, Naomi hadn't been much better when she and Clay were dating.

"I'm working really hard on keeping my grades up," Clay told Mira. "I don't ever want to lose my eligibility to play football again."

"The Chavez Cougars need you, babe," Mira told him. "When you weren't playing, they were just dismal. You're the heart of the team. You're such a leader, Clay. The other guys really look up to you. That game Friday night when you had the pass interception, that was awesome!"

"It feels great to bring in a win," Clay declared. He was soaking up Mira's adoration like a dog lapping water on a hot day.

"I bet you play in the NFL someday, Clay," Mira oozed. "Maybe you'll take your team to the Super Bowl."

"That's my dream, girl," Clay declared. "I'm hoping I get a football scholarship to a good college. Then I could be drafted by maybe the Chargers. Oh, by the way, Mira, that book report Hunt wants. You done with that?"

Naomi shuddered. She remembered how she used to do Clay's schoolwork for him when they were dating. Naomi felt awful about doing that. She felt she was helping Clay cheat. But he told her it was the only way he could keep his grades up. So she ignored her conscience and did his work for him. Naomi remembered a very ugly incident when she did his paper for him but forgot to bring it in the morning it was due. Clay screamed at her, calling her many horrible names. Ernesto had been in that class. He looked shocked and disgusted by how Clay was treating her. Naomi didn't even know Ernesto then, but his look of compassion for her touched her heart.

"Oh," Mira replied, "I didn't get to it, babe. When's it due again?" Mira didn't seem too concerned.

"It's due tomorrow, stupid," Clay barked. His sweet, lovable manner toward Mira changed in an instant. His reaction brought back bad memories for Naomi. Clay could be so endearing, so charming. But if you crossed him, he turned into a rude creep. Ugly insults flew from his lips. Naomi was sick at the memory of the many times Clay called her "stupid." Now, looking back at that time, she could hardly believe she put up with him for so long.

Ever since Naomi was a little girl, she heard her father direct words like "dummy" and "stupid" at her mother. Naomi knew that Dad loved Mom. Yet he was often rude. He hurt her again and again with ugly insults. Now Dad was much better with Mom, but the rude behavior had gone on for a long time. Naomi thought maybe that set her up for accepting Clay Aguirre for so long. Naomi didn't understand that it was wrong for guys to put girls and women down. Words, she knew now, could have a terrible impact.

Naomi wondered whether the situation in Mira's home was like hers had been. Maybe Mira's Mom wasn't respected.

"I'll do the report tonight, Clay," Mira promised. "I'll get right at it. I'll have it done for tomorrow in class." Mira sounded contrite and anxious.

"You'll do a rotten job rushing like that," Clay fumed. "Hunt'll give me a low grade. How can you be such an idiot, Mira? You *know* how much it means to me to get a good grade in English. I can't believe you're so stupid. You put off doing the report. Now you're gonna rush through it and do a lousy job."

Mira started to cry. "Oh Clay, I forgot. I've got a big project in science, and I had to do that. Your report just slipped my mind."

Sherry and Naomi exchanged disgusted looks. Sherry looked like the kind of a girl who wouldn't take much from a guy.

"What if I flunk English and get kicked off the football team again, stupid? It'll be your fault," Clay raged. "Come on, let's get out of here, you idiot!"

They left their yogurt half eaten and rushed out the door. Naomi heard Ernesto's Volvo, and she went off shift.

As she went out the back door and it slammed shut behind her, she saw the BMW coming to a stop.

CHAPTER TEN

Naomi thought briefly of running around the building to the front of Chill Out. But she didn't. Ernesto's Volvo was pulling into the lot. She decided to jump into the car, and they'd get out of here. Naomi kept telling herself everything would be okay. Mr. Ancho had just come by to see his son. The man might wave to Naomi and say hello, as he did the other night. He was very cordial then, and he would be now. She had nothing to worry about. Naomi told herself not to overreact.

Ernesto had seen the BMW too, and he was out of his car. Naomi walked quickly to his side, her heart pounding. She kept telling herself that her fear was irrational and ridiculous. But she was still fearful. The moment Naomi reached Ernesto, he slipped his arm around her shoulders protectively. Ernesto looked tense, and the sight of that made Naomi even more nervous. "Let's just get outta here," he said.

They moved toward the Volvo. Ernesto followed Naomi toward the passenger side to let her in. He planned to rush to the driver's side, get in, and lock the car from the inside. Then they would take off before Mr. Ancho was out of the BMW. That was the plan.

But it didn't work. Mr. Ancho was out of his BMW, and he blocked Naomi's path to the Volvo.

"Hi Mr. Ancho," Naomi greeted him in a shaky voice. "My dad enjoyed meeting you the other night. Uh . . . was Mexico good? That's such a beautiful country."

Mr. Ancho was staring at Ernesto with narrow, grim eyes. Then he looked at Naomi. "Is this punk bothering you?" he demanded.

"No, no," Naomi gasped, her legs turning weak. "Everything's fine."

Ernesto put his arm around Naomi's shoulders again, pulling her close to him.

"Take your hands off my wife," Mr. Ancho commanded in a menacing voice. "Alexa, he has no right to put his arm around you like that."

Naomi thought she might faint. She leaned against Ernesto for support. She glanced at the back door of Chill Out. She hoped against hope that it would open and that Jimmy would come running out to take control of his father. But the green door remained tightly shut.

"Mr. Ancho," Naomi stated as calmly as she could, "I'm Naomi Martinez. I work at the yogurt place, Chill Out. Your son Jimmy hired me. This is my boyfriend, Ernesto. He goes to Chavez High with me." Naomi was trying desperately to snap the man back to reality.

"I don't know what you're talking about, Alexa," Mr. Ancho responded.

"Falling off the boat has unhinged your mind. You're not making sense. But I knew all along you didn't drown. They tried to tell me you drowned. I love you so much, Alexa. I would have known in my heart if you were dead. I knew you were alive. And here you are, more beautiful than ever."

Mr. Ancho took a step toward Naomi. Ernesto's arm tightened on her shoulders. "Come with me, Alexa," the man said. "We'll drive somewhere and have one of those wonderful French dinners you love so much. Do you remember saying that no one can cook like the French, darling?"

Naomi glanced at Ernesto. He was reaching for his cell phone to call 9-1-1. But Mr. Ancho saw what he was doing. The older man warned Ernesto. "Do not try to call some of your evil friends to come and help you abduct my wife. I have a gun if you or anyone else tries to stop us, you little punk."

Before they could react, Mr. Ancho was pointing a small pistol at them. "You've done enough damage already," he told them. "I believe you were the one who abducted my darling from the ship. Then you made it look like she had fallen overboard, just so you could have her. You won't get away with taking her again. My wife and I are getting into my car and leaving now. Come Alexa."

Naomi was horrified to see the gun in Mr. Ancho's hand. Ernesto's mind was racing to think of something he could do without placing Naomi in harm's way.

"I am not afraid to use this gun," the man threatened.

Naomi cast another desperate glance at the back door of Chill Out. If only somebody would look out the window and see what was happening. "Please," she prayed under her breath. "Please, somebody come out and help us!"

"Alexa," Mr. Ancho directed, "I want you to get into our BMW now. There it is, right over there. Walk over to the car and get in. If this punk makes a move to stop you,

I will shoot him. Remember, darling, when we bought this car? You were so delighted to be riding in a BMW. We have a wonderful life ahead of us, Alexa. Nobody is going to keep us apart again. Now go to the car."

Naomi's gaze swept the dark parking lot. Nobody was around. All the customers were gone, and both Sherry and Jimmy were parked in the front lot.

The light showing through the bottom of the back door dimmed. Jimmy and Sherry were closing the store. They were locking the back door from the inside, going out the front door, and never looking back. Seconds later, Naomi and Ernesto heard two cars start up in the front lot. And they heard the cars drive away.

Sherry and Jimmy had no idea what was happening just outside the back door.

Mr. Ancho waved the pistol, "Go to the car now, Alexa," he commanded. "Are you afraid of this punk, Alexa? Is that why you won't get into the car? Don't be afraid. I'll shoot him if he tries to stop you."

If Naomi got into the BMW, she wondered whether she'd ever get out alive. Mr. Ancho thought she was Alexa. Why would he harm the woman he thought was his wife? Still, the police always warned women never to get into an abductor's car, no matter what. Once the abductor had someone in the car, she was helpless. Anything would be better than being in the BMW with that man, Naomi thought. She would rather be shot where she stood than to get into the car.

Suddenly, without warning, Ernesto pushed Naomi hard. She dropped to her knees in the grass alongside the parking lot. Mr. Ancho aimed his gun as Ernesto lunged at him. The gun went off, and acrid smoke filled the air. Naomi began screaming as she grabbed her cell phone and punched in 9-1-1. She gasped out Chill Out's address. "A madman is in the back lot with a gun!" Naomi screamed into the phone. "He's shooting!"

Naomi got to her feet to see Ernesto and Ancho struggling for the gun. It went off again. Naomi saw the flash and screamed in terror. Had Ernesto been hit? In the darkness she couldn't see. Two dark figures struggled in the shadows until one of them fell backward. Naomi heard the sickening knock of a skull on the blacktop.

She rushed toward the dark figure that had dropped to his knees. It was Ernesto. A few feet away, Mr. Ancho lay on the asphalt. The gun had been dropped somewhere in the darkness. The whole struggle had taken only seconds.

"Ernie!" Naomi sobbed, clutching at him. "Ernie! Are you all right?"

"I'm okay. I'm okay, babe," Ernesto assured her, taking Naomi in his arms. She was shaking badly. Not even his arms around her could keep her still.

"I was lucky, babe," Ernesto told her in a shaky voice. "Really lucky. I was able to grab his arm and force the gun upward. Both shots went wild. Scared the heck outta me, though. Man, he's strong for an old guy. I wasn't sure I could take him. But then I got a solid punch in, and he fell backward. I don't know where the gun is. I guess we should try to find it."

Naomi didn't care about the gun. She clung to him tightly. They could hear sirens getting louder.

Mr. Ancho was coming to, mumbling incoherently. The only words Naomi could make out were, "Alexa? . . . Alexa?" He rolled over and got up on his hands and knees. Blood ran down his cheek from a nasty wound on the back of his head. He collapsed to ground, face down.

A police car rolled to stop about ten yards away from the three people. The siren was off, but the lights were still flashing. Two officers jumped out. From the protection of the patrol car doors, they yelled, "Everyone stand up. Put your hands in the air where we can see them." They shouted the instructions over and over.

Ernesto and Naomi stood up right away, their hands raised. The officers came up to them slowly, from different directions.

Their weapons were pointed at all three people—Ernesto, Naomi, and Mr. Ancho.

One officer patted Ernesto down and called for a female backup. The other officer approached Mr. Ancho and called for EMTs. By this time, two more police cars had arrived. The officers holstered their weapons.

"Okay," the first officer asked, "what's goin' on here?"

"The man there on the ground," Ernesto explained. "He's outta his mind. He tried to kidnap my girlfriend. Thought she was his wife. He had a gun. We had a fight, and the gun went flyin'. I think it's on the grass over there."

"He's crazy!" Naomi sobbed. "His wife died, and he thinks I'm her. He wanted to kidnap me, but Ernie here saved me. He . . . almost . . . almost got shot saving me."

The officers recovered Mr. Ancho's gun. The EMT vehicle was easing its way into the lot. The officer turned his flashlight on the two kids. Ernesto's forehead sported a large bump that was growing and turning dark.

"How'd you get that lump," the officer asked him.

Ernesto touched a couple of fingers to his forehead. He'd not been aware of the lump. "Guess I got it when we knocked heads," he replied.

"Want the EMTs to look at it, son?" the officer suggested.

"Nah, thanks. I'm okay," Ernesto answered.

Ernesto then was asked to describe exactly what happened. He told the story from the time Naomi left the store to when the cops arrived. Naomi nodded agreement with what he said and gave the officer Jimmy's cell phone number. Ernesto ended his account by saying, "No way was I gonna let my girl in the car with that nut job. I had to tackle him, or he would have taken Naomi away."

"You tackled an armed man, huh, kid?" the officer asked, shaking his head. "This is

187

your lucky night, kid. You gambled and you won."

"No way was he gonna take Naomi," Ernesto said again. He was still breathing hard from the adrenalin rush. Naomi was at his side, his arm around her shoulders.

Naomi and Ernesto gave the police officer all their contact information. The officer glanced over to Mr. Ancho, still lying on the ground. Two EMTs were giving him first aid. "Well," the office explained, "I'm not sure what kind of story we'll get from him." The officer nodded in the direction of Mr. Ancho. "Just stay here for now. Let me call this Jimmy." And he walked away.

The officer was back with them in a few minutes. "Okay," he said, "Jimmy's on the way. He confirmed everything about his father. He's on the way over. Said to tell you he was very sorry about all this."

"He'll want to be with his father right away," Naomi said, only now calming down.

"We may be contacting you later on," the officer advised. "Do you guys need help getting home?"

"No," Ernesto declined. "I'll just drive Naomi home and go home myself. Thanks."

"I just want to go home," Naomi stammered, still shaken.

"You sure you're up to taking her and yourself home?" the officer asked in a kindly voice, seeing that the pair were just teenagers.

"Yes," Ernesto assured him. "We live very close to here."

As the Volvo pulled slowly from the parking lot of Chill Out, Naomi's head was on Ernesto's shoulder.

"Ernie, you saved me," Naomi kept saying, over and over. "You went up against a man with a gun to save me."

"No babe, I saved myself," Ernesto said. "Without you, I'd be no good. No good at all."

By now, it was ten thirty, and Naomi called her house.

"Naomi," Felix Martinez cried. "You okay? What's the matter? Me and your mom been worried sick."

"I'm okay, Daddy," Naomi assured him. "I'll be home in a few minutes with Ernie. We're both okay. We'll explain when we get there."

Then Naomi called the Sandoval house.

Maria Sandoval answered. "Yes?" she said in a tense voice. The Sandovals had been worried too.

"Mrs. Sandoval, this is Naomi," the girl said.

"Naomi, you sound terrible!" Mrs. Sandoval exclaimed. "Is everything all right? Ernesto said he'd be home at nine fifteen after taking you home. Is he all right, Naomi?"

"Ernesto is driving me home right now," Naomi told her. "We're going to my house."

"We'll meet you there," Mrs. Sandoval said.

Ernesto drove into the driveway of the Martinez house on Bluebird Street. Only seconds later, Luis and Maria Sandoval pulled in behind them. Both the Sandovals jumped from their car and rushed toward them. As they did, Felix and Linda Martinez burst from the house. Even Brutus, barking loudly, joined in.

Naomi was crying. Her parents put their arms around her and led her into the house. "Hey, baby," Felix Martinez whispered. "Take it easy . . . take it easy."

They all gathered in the kitchen, where Linda Martinez poured hot coffee. Naomi was so shaken she could hardly speak. All she managed to say was, "This madman, he tried to kidnap me. He had a gun, and Ernie saved me. He went up against a guy with a loaded gun to save me."

Ernesto explained what had happened while both sets of parents listened. "I couldn't let him take Naomi," he concluded, "I couldn't let that happen."

"You went after a guy with a gun!" Felix Martinez gasped with awe in his voice. Mr. Martinez had always thought

Ernesto was a nice kid but a wimp. The man had not given Ernesto much credit in the courage department. Now, except for this kid, Felix Martinez's sixteen-year-old daughter would be missing somewhere with a madman.

"I had to," Ernesto asserted. "I couldn't let him take her."

Ernesto was suddenly exhausted. He had been running on nervous energy— adrenalin—until this point. Now he felt he as though he was going to collapse.

As the Sandovals got up to go, Felix Martinez walked over to Ernesto. The man threw his arms around Ernesto and gave him a hug that almost took the boy's breath away.

"Boy," he declared in a husky voice, "I had three sons, but that ain't the way it is no more. I got four sons now. Luis Sandoval and Maria, you guys got to share Ernie with me. From this day on, I love him like my own blood. Far as I'm concerned, Ernie, what you done for my little girl tonight, you're family. You're blood."

Ernesto thanked Mr. Martinez and mumbled, "I only did what I had to do." Mr. Sandoval shook Felix's hand and said goodnight. Mrs. Sandoval followed her husband and son out the door. Ernesto kissed Naomi and gave her a final hug.

The boy left in his Volvo with his father driving. Maria Sandoval drove the family minivan home. When Ernesto got home, he collapsed into bed.

In the morning, Naomi got a call from Jimmy Ancho. He said his father was in a high-security mental health facility. He might be facing charges of attempted kidnap and attempted murder. Given his mental state, a plea of insanity was probable. If the DA did not bring charges, it would be only if Jimmy's father was kept locked up in a hospital by court order. Either way, Elia Ancho would not be on the outside anytime soon. Jimmy Ancho sounded brokenhearted. He kept saying to Naomi, over and over, "I am so sorry. I am sorry beyond words."

"It wasn't your fault," Naomi assured him. "We're praying for you and your father."

Orlando and Manny Martinez came over that weekend to help Naomi prepare to play Dolores Huerta. The Cesar Chavez birthday celebration was on for the following Friday night at the high school that bore the name of the activist.

That night, Naomi was feeling pretty confident as she stood in the spotlight. She sang beautifully, as Dolores Huerta, about the children of the farmworkers. Ernesto delivered stirring speeches by Cesar Chavez. And a chorus of students carried the union flag with the black eagle and the banner of Our Lady of Guadalupe. The flag and banner had been at all of Chavez's marches.

The players took their final bows to thunderous applause. When Naomi looked out into the audience, she saw her parents and her three brothers. Felix Martinez was on his feet, clapping with his hands in the air over his head. He couldn't have been more excited if one of his boys had won the Super Bowl.

All the Sandovals came, including *Abuela* Lena and Ernesto's little sisters, Katalina and Juanita. Even Mom's parents from Los Angeles came. Hortencia came with Oscar Perez. Oscar had mentioned that he would like to talk to Naomi about joining his band. All Luis Sandoval's siblings and their spouses came.

After the school celebration, some of the evening was left. Naomi and Ernesto climbed into his Volvo and sneaked off together. The Sandoval and Martinez families saw the two making their getaway. They smiled and approved of it. Naomi and Ernesto deserved some time alone together.

The day had been warm and windy. Now the night sky was filled with countless stars sprinkled across the darkness. In her life, Naomi had never seen so many stars.

They drove to the ocean. They often went to a certain place on hot days, to swim in the water and lie on the sand. But it was too cool to do that tonight. They walked down a broad, smooth path to the sand. Naomi had brought a blanket and a thick beach towel. They sat on the towel, with the blanket around both their shoulders. They looked out to the sea. The pounding of the waves echoed in their hearts.

Both of them were lost in their thoughts, but slowly they turned to face each other. Ernesto cupped his hands around Naomi's face. He gently kissed her brow, the tip of her nose, and finally her lips. They held their kiss for a long time. They held hands and stared upward at the beautiful dark sky.

Ernesto had thought, months ago, that he could not love Naomi more than he did then. But now he loved her even more. He loved her so much, he felt almost overwhelmed. He recalled that terrible moment when he thought he might lose her. He'd stood in that dark parking lot. He'd seen the gun in the sick man's hand, seen the man's determination to take Naomi away. At that terrible moment, he realized just how much he loved her.

Naomi's love for Ernesto had grown slowly. But tonight it blazed, brightly. She could not imagine living without him.

"Love you babe, love you forever," Ernesto whispered.

"Forever and ever," Naomi responded.

They sat side by side on the sand for a long while. They listened to the surf crashing on the beach. They stared silently at the dark ocean.

Ernesto felt good about the performance. He believed he had done well, and he knew Naomi was a hit as Dolores Huerta. He thought the theme of the show somehow fit his mood. But he wasn't sure how. He was searching for a word to describe how he felt. Then it came to him.

Deliverance.

Cesar Chavez had devoted his life to the deliverance of his people. Ernesto felt that he had somehow been delivered too—from Felix Martinez. Ernesto grinned in the darkness at the thought. Maybe, Ernesto thought, he was being too dramatic. But he was very happy that Naomi's dad accepted him now. Yes, that was his deliverance.

Most important of all, Naomi had been saved from the hands of a madman. Ernesto forced himself not to think about what might have happened. Hers was a true deliverance.

Ernesto looked over at Naomi's beautiful face gleaming in the moonlight. He had no words explain what he was thinking or how he felt. He just reached over and took her hand in his.